Blissful Surrender

BJ Harvey

DEDICATION

To Nikki aka Bulldog

You're the bestest friend I've never met.

My rock, my cheerleader, my motivator and most

importantly a dear friend.

Sean will always be yours now ;)

CONTENTS

PROLOGUE – "BAD DAY"

Sean

I'm not one who is easily rattled.

In fact, my cage is so secure it might as well be anchored to the ground in concrete. It's why I'm so damn good at what I do—corporate law. 'The Shark' is what they call me. I revel in it, thrive under pressure. In fact, cool, calm and collected should be my middle names.

Then, like the flip of a coin, there is the other half of my life. The side that isn't so organized. My personal life, the part of my life that should be under control, is a clusterfuck right now. And as always, it all points to one person.

By day, I'm like Teflon—shit doesn't stick to me. I don't let it. My work doesn't get brought home. It starts and ends at my office door. Just the way I like it.

I should be sitting back in my soft leather recliner, drinking a well-earned glass of Macallan on ice. So why am I sitting in front of a computer screen watching security footage of my younger brother Ryan handing an envelope to an unknown man at the club?

My fucking club.

Thankfully, the video I'm watching isn't a live feed. That would have been too much for me to handle. I have a pretty controlled temperament, but I'd be barreling down there and punching him in the face, then kicking his useless ass to the curb once and for all. Instead, I'm watching delayed footage from yesterday afternoon that my private investigator sent me.

Blood or not, nobody fucks me over. I suspect Ryan is putting the club and me on someone's unwelcome radar, and I don't need the attention or the bullshit. Yes, I know the fact that I have a PI watching my own brother speaks volumes. Ryan is a gullible son of a bitch with a magnet for assholes and trouble in equal measure. As soon as I had an inkling that he was involved in dodgy shit (again), I asked my friend Asher to step in and monitor the situation for me. It was a necessary step to take. He fucked up two months ago and I stood by him but now … well, enough is enough.

CHAPTER 1: "TROUBLE"

Sean

Let me explain how we got to this point. A quick run down memory lane, so to speak.

My name is Sean Edward Miller, first born son to Harvey and Annette Miller. Two years later, Ryan Anthony Miller was born. Two rambunctious sons who were very much wanted and loved by our parents. My brother and I were born into privilege, not wanting for anything. Unfortunately, this only exacerbated my brother's sense of entitlement. Even at a young age, Ryan had a love for money and wealth rarely seen in a young boy.

When we were twelve and ten, our parents were killed in a carjacking. I still remember the day the police came to the door with our grandfather who had flown in from Chicago. They took us into the living room and told us that our parents had been killed and that we'd have to go live with our grandparents in Chicago.

Although it was twenty-one years ago, I still remember that day like it was yesterday. The soft floral scent of my mother's perfume that filled the room as she was getting ready for a fundraising event in the city. The look of awe in my father's eyes as he watched my mother walk down the stairs with poise and grace. The love poured into the kiss goodbye that she gave both of her sons as she left, and the smile my father gave us as they waved and walked out the front door, telling us they'd see us soon.

But it wasn't just another night.

Those are the last memories I have of my parents being alive. It's a moment forever burned into my subconscious and has been the driving force in my life ever since. Everything I've achieved, and everything I've ever done is for my parents. I've wanted to lead a successful, happy and fulfilled life in their honor, and I like to think I've achieved that so far.

Ryan was affected in far deeper ways than I was and as much as I try to help him, he just can't seem to stay on the straight and narrow, so I keep bailing him out of trouble. I'm his safety net.

I pull off my tie that hangs limp around my neck before undoing my platinum cufflinks and dropping them onto my antique Chinese Elm desk. Pausing the video, I leave the office and make my way through my dark, empty condo to the living room, the sound of footsteps bouncing off the walls, echoing through the air. Stopping in front of my drinks cabinet, I wrap my hands around the crystal decanter of whisky that's calling my name and pour three fingers into the matching glass—a wedding gift that belonged to my parents and a rare antique that my brother has always coveted. Knocking back the burning amber liquid, I pour myself another, drinking it down as quickly as the first. The burning sensation in my chest eases into a nice warmth that quickly spreads throughout my tension-filled body. I pour a glass again, this time walking over to the refrigerator and adding two ice cubes before turning on a few lights in the living area and returning to my office.

I sit down in front of the paused screen and push play, watching in slow motion as my brother appears to pay someone off. It's all assumption and hearsay at the moment. But an empty club plus a bulging envelope being handed over to a stranger who does NOT look like a banker or a security guard … well, it doesn't look good does it?

And it was all done while I was ten blocks away in my tall glass building, knee deep in a hostile takeover mediation. Who knew the real hostility was being carried out in my own backyard?

As I take another sip of my drink and I watch another camera angle of the 'transaction', the sick feeling in my stomach increases. He has not only involved himself in the shit this time, he's dragged my ass into his mess. The shit that my brother attracts just never fucking ends.

If my father or grandfather were alive today, they'd have me tanning his hide and throwing him out on his ear. But I can't seem to do that. Every single fucking time I save the day. As much as I try to clear the way for him to stay legit and finally make something of himself he always stumbles. Despite the time, effort and many opportunities afforded to him by me, nothing seems to change.

Well, this time it's going to be different.

Once I've calmed down enough to talk to him, I'll make him understand that this time he's gone too far.

This time he's going to have to learn the hard way.

Alone.

Sam

Two Days Later

"Roberts, get your ass over here. Stop mooning over your fiancée or I'll have you written up sooner than you can say yes ma'am." I try to keep a straight face but on the inside I'm having trouble backing up my threats. He knows as well as I do that when it comes to Zander, I seem to lose my ice queen tag.

Zander Roberts has been my partner for six months and in that time he's managed to do what many before him have failed at—loosen me up. I've been, for lack of a better word, uptight for the best part of a decade. In order to be the strong, capable and independent woman my mother raised me to be, I've had to wear what I now liken to being my invisible armor— impenetrable to anyone and anything. I've been all about the job. First the academy, then working on the street doing general patrol and a field training officer. Zander was the last recruit I took on as a field training officer. I worked him to the bone for a month while he experienced what the reality of being a cop in Chicago entailed. And he did me proud. So much so that I requested he become my partner when I returned to patrol.

Now, we're as tight as partners can be. He still has his moments where he drives me insane, but all in all he's professional and alert and there is no one else who I'd rather have my back.

I hear the computer in the patrol car ding and with the press of a button I see a call come up for an assault at an address in the club district. Division Street to be exact. My body goes cold when I realize what club it is.

Dammit. Shit, damn, mother-fucking hell. Why me!

Zander looks over at me and quirks a brow. "Sam, you think we might get moving? You're just sitting there staring at the screen. Is there a problem?"

I shake my head to snap myself out of it. I can do this. I'm a professional. I'm a freaking cop for Christ's sake. I can walk into that club—an establishment that, in itself, I despise— and do my job. Yes, I can be Samantha Richards, policewoman and servant to the city of Chicago.

"Sam?"

I move into action.

Flicking the lights and sirens on, I turn the key in the ignition, then clear my throat and lick my lips which have suddenly gone dry as a fucking desert. "I'm good, Roberts. We're good. Let's get this done. Can you keep an eye out for the bus? We'll need to make sure the scene is safe for them before they can go in."

"Sure thing."

Three minutes later and I'm slamming to a stop outside a large, black, concrete building with the word Throb painted large and proud in bright red writing across the front. It's bold, daring, and proud ... just like the club owner himself. Fuck! No, do not think about him.

Zander and I get out of our patrol car just as the ambulance pulls up behind us and I see my best friends Heather and Rico jump out then walk around the back of the bus to get ready. Checking that Zander has my back, I draw my weapon from the belt at my hip.

Together we walk into the club, taking a careful step inside. "CPD, is anyone in here?"

"H-Help! I need help!" a raspy voice shouts in desperation from the back of the large dance floor.

Zander runs ahead, weapon back in his holster. "Roberts, fucking hold up, will you? Have you cleared the scene? Think about your own back, and mine for that matter, before anything else. God, have I taught you nothing?" Zander's good but he still has his green moments. Now being one of them.

He stops in his tracks and turns his head to look at me. "Dammit, he needs help, Sam."

"I know, but right now I don't care. We're no use to him if we get attacked, are we?" I raise an eyebrow to him as I look around the room, scanning for anything or anyone out of the ordinary. Standing back, I'm still unable to see the victim.

"Is he still here, sir? Are you alone?"

"Y-Yeah," he sputters out. "The guy that … uh, roughed me up some left through the back when he heard sirens."

"Robbery?"

"Uh … yeah. It must've been."

Suddenly I'm suspicious and there's a knot forming in my stomach. A robbery of a nightclub in the early afternoon? Something isn't right here.

"He didn't get anything," he continues, his voice getting stronger the more he talks. He sounds more sure of himself now; a complete one-eighty from when we first arrived. "The safe needs double verification and my brother seems to have changed the combination overnight without telling me."

With Zander at my side, we both move quickly toward his voice. Once happy that the room is secure, I yell, "CLEAR!" toward the front doors, hoping the two officers out on the street hear me. "Where are you, sir?" I ask when I reach the bar. I look over and see a familiar man slumped against the fridges lining the back wall.

"Ryan?" I say in shock, my voice hoarse. I put my arm on the bar and push my body up and over, using my legs as leverage.

"Sammy? Fuck!" He falls sideways, but I manage to catch his head before it hits the hard tiled floor. I slide down to the floor and lean back against the wall, resting Ryan's head in my lap. His right eye is almost swollen shut and I see a cut to his cheek that doesn't look too deep but is slowly oozing blood.

"Roberts, go get the paramedics. He needs help," I yell to Zander who is coming through the side of the bar to join us.

"On it. You okay here?"

"Yep. Go get them, Zander. Now!"

"Can't … tell … Sean …" he whispers, his eye closing.

I shake him, trying to keep him awake. He may have a concussion. "Stop, Ryan. Where are you hurt?" I run my hand over his head, flinching when I feel the familiar warm sticky feeling of blood and matted hair between my fingers. Guaranteed head injury.

"He jumped … me … in my own fucking bar. Sean's going to be so—"

"No, Ryan, don't worry about that right now. Where else?"

"What?" He looks up at me in confusion.

"Where else are you hurt?" I question.

"Ribs," he wheezes. "The fucker kicked me in the ribs, then knocked my head against the wall."

I see Helen and Rico round the bar. I look up and give them a grim smile. They're my best friends and just happen to be the paramedics on duty today. To be honest, it's nice to see a friendly face given that I'm scared shitless that a man I've tried to forget for the past ten years could make an appearance at any moment. I look down at Ryan again and see his dark, sapphire blue eyes looking back up at me like I'm his hero or something. With his guard down, I catch a glimpse of the lost little boy from all those years ago; the man who never quite recovered from the tragedy of his past. It hurts my soul just as much now as it did back then. Losing your parents, and then losing your grandparents eight years later would have an effect on even the strongest man. Like Sean …

I take a deep breath and swallow down the lump in my throat. "Ryan, the paramedics are here to look after you now." I hold my hands up as he is pulled off me, then push off the floor and stand up, stepping out of the bar area to give them space to check him over. I look down at my previously clean blue shirt and see a large, crimson blood stain.

Dammit all to Hell. I've still got half a shift left.

Walking aimlessly through the room, I shake my head in disbelief. Ryan fucking Miller. The younger brother of the one man I'd ever let close enough to shatter me. At this moment, I hate and love his brother all over again.

Sean Miller.

The biggest sacrifice of my life.

The one I let go.

Fuck! I need to get out of here before Sean shows up and my day goes to complete shit.

Then it hits me. With Ryan gone, there will be no one here, and if it was a robbery, there is nothing to stop the dickhead returning. Without thinking of the consequences for myself, I spin on my heels and head back toward Ryan. This is totally above and beyond the call of duty and I know it.

"Ry, is there anyone else here today? Anyone else working who can close up for you?"

"Nah. Sean's not due in for another hour because of some deposition he's involved with, and Amy, our other bar manager, is due around the same time."

Fuck. Shit. Christ Almighty.

I look to the ceiling, begging whichever higher being watching over me to take me then and there.

"Where are your keys, Ryan?"

"Back pocket. Jeans," he rasps out, his voice muffled by the oxygen mask now covering his mouth. Rico looks up at me and raises his eyebrow. I nod and watch as he reaches inside Ryan's pocket, pulling out a foot long chain with a stack of keys attached. He makes sure he unclips the chain from Ryan's jeans before throwing them my way.

Rico and I tried to date a few years ago, and although it didn't work out, we've been close friends ever since. He's Brazilian and all kinds of hot. Chocolate brown hair, deep green eyes, and a body that is a masterpiece of sculpted lines and hard muscle. One look at him and you can tell how much time and effort he puts into it. Helen is his partner and fiancée. She's my complete opposite with black hair cut into a jagged, almost razor edge style that not a lot of women could pull off, but she rocks it, big brown eyes that are beautiful and captivating, and a unique style that she dons proudly—in and out of uniform.

They may be partners but Rico and Helen are also a couple. When they tried the dating thing a year ago—after I insisted— they hit it off like a space rocket on launch day. Sparks flew, clothes ripped off, and they're getting married next year. I couldn't be happier for them.

As I turn toward the club's front doors and reach up to grab my radio, Zander walks in.

"Roberts, can you—"

"Tape is up and two rookies are still outside guarding the door. I scoped out the neighbors on either side. They heard shouting, and one called 911 but didn't see anyone leave. Detectives are on the way, but I doubt we'll find whoever did this. I came through the back door and there's a small alleyway behind this block. I'd say the perp escaped that way. Once that guy is patched up they'll be able to interview him and get access to the security tapes. Get a better look."

I look up at my partner and narrow my eyes. "You did all of that since you went outside?"

He grins his 'I'm shit hot and I know it' look that he's famous for around the precinct. The former stripper in him shines through as he turns on the charm. "Of course, partner. That's what you wanted me to do, isn't it?"

"Piss off, Roberts. Your bullshit charm won't work on me."

"It's worked before," he retorts with a cheeky grin.

"Got your sights set on making Detective, Zan?" I reply back, smirking at him. My partner has come a long way in a few months. It's great to see him taking initiative.

"One day."

"It's good to have a goal in life beyond being really, really good looking" I retort with a smirk. "Anyway, let's lock up and leave the keys with the officers out front until the other owner arrives," I state, my cop persona snapping back into place.

"Return of the Ice Queen," he mumbles under his breath.

"Say what now?"

He rubs the back of his neck as Rico and Helen wheel Ryan's stretcher past us. Helen mouths 'Are you okay?' as they head toward the door, and I nod. It's a white lie I know she'll call me out on later, but at least it will be when I'm at home with a gin and tonic in my hand and not in the fetish club that my ex-boyfriend owns.

"Zander," I say quietly once the paramedics and Ryan are gone. "I'm called the Ice Queen?"

His eyes soften. "Sam, it's just a stupid name. Just ignore it."

I think on it for a moment before I shock the shit out of him by replying with a shit eating grin on my face. "I'm disappointed. I thought for sure I'd be known as a ball buster. I'll have to try harder."

He cracks up laughing before giving me a shoulder bump. We walk out the front doors, pulling them closed before securing the club. I throw the keys at Officer Keats who is standing by our patrol car. "Keats, Detectives will be here soon. When Sean Miller or a bar manager named Amy arrive, please tell them what has happened and give Mr. Miller those keys. I'll get the detectives to keep trying to get through to him as well. Any problems, call it in."

When Zander and I are back in the squad car and he's called through our clear status over the radio, he turns in the passenger seat and stares at me, studying me quietly. The silence stretches between us, and suddenly I'm feeling awkward and uncomfortable. I've never liked people getting involved in my personal business. I'm a very private person and he knows it. We may be partners, but I won't be talking about Sean Miller and our history with Zander. Not now when it's suddenly being refreshed in my mind, and not ever.

"Roberts, cut the shit. Let's go," I say, crossing my arms and leveling an equally unimpressed stare right back at him.

"You know him, don't you?"

I look up at him and there's concern written all over his face. "Yes. He's an old … friend's brother. I'm okay, Zander. It's not the brother that's the problem," I confess, knowing I've said too much, but unable to stop myself.

"Then it's the ex? Because if so, you need to be off this case now. Any connection is too much."

"Is that what happened when Kate needed you?" I retort bitchily, instantly regretting the words the moment they leave my mouth.

For a brief moment, he looks taken aback by my comment, but he cools his response immediately. "Sure, Sam, I hear you. But I don't understand the weird vibe I'm getting from you or why you'd be uncomfortable in that club." He jerks his head toward Throb without taking his eyes off me. "Since you know Ryan and we're quiet right now, do you want to head over to Northwestern and check in on him?"

I shake my head from side to side. I don't need to get involved in Ryan's mess this time. It's not my place. It's never been my place. Just like his brother has no place in my head. It's ancient history, and just an unfortunate coincidence that our lives have inadvertently collided twice in as many months. I'll just rack it up to being bad luck and keep Sean out of my head.

Lucky for me, I'm yet to set eyes on the very man who marked me all those years ago. The man who has the power to bring me to my knees, in all ways possible.

Somehow I don't think luck is going to be on my side for much longer after today.

CHAPTER 2 – "SAFE & SOUND"

Sean

After spending all afternoon in a deposition that went way over time, I'm finally back in my office looking at a stack of messages my secretary has left on my desk and contemplating another long night ahead of me. It's already 4 p.m., but I've still got half a day's work to catch up on.

I spin my silver watch on my wrist, a habit of mine when I'm frustrated. The engraving on the back of it is forever engrained in my memory.

To the best man I know and the only man I'll love.

It was my mother's last Christmas gift she gave my father before they died and it has taken pride of place on my left hand. My grandfather gave it to me when the movers were packing up our old house in New York. He said, "Boy, one day you're going to grow up to be a man, and then you'll meet the one woman who will cut you off at the knees and realize that you willingly let her every time. When that happens, I want you to remember the love your parents had. It was an enduring love, the everlasting, all-encompassing kind that I know all about. When you find that, Sean, you grab hold tight and never let go."

I snap out of my walk down memory lane and undo the top button of my shirt, running my fingers under my tie and loosening the knot I'd made this morning. I may like suits, but ties are my downfall. I only wear them for as long as absolutely necessary.

Pulling my phone out of my pocket, I look at the screen and grimace. My phone has been vibrating for the past hour, but unfortunately, this is the first chance I've had to check it. Three calls from the club, and at least four more from an unknown number. What the hell is going on? I shouldn't be getting any calls from the club unless the place is burning down, and if Ryan really needs me he calls me from his cell. I don't feel like speaking to him anyway. I'd likely say something I'd regret and he'd go on a bender again. And right now, that's the last thing either of us needs.

I ring the club and Amy answers. "Throb, Amy speaking."

"Amy, It's Sean. Do you know why I've had so many calls from—"

"Sean! Oh my god! Have you spoken to Ryan yet? Is he okay?" She's talking a million miles an hour and isn't making sense.

"Okay Amy, slow down. Where's Ryan?"

"Oh shit, you don't know? Ryan was attacked in the club today during a robbery. He was knocked around a bit, so he was taken to hospital about two hours ago." I hear her take a deep breath, obviously trying to calm herself down.

"He what?" I'm in shock. I have to be. There is no way anyone would rob the club in the middle of the damn day. That's ballsy and stupid, and simply fucked up.

"He was beat up by a robber. There were cops here when I arrived to start prepping for tonight."

"What hospital, Amy?"

"Northwestern."

"Okay. Do you need someone to cover?"

"Already sorted, boss. Isabel came in. She was happy to."

"Good." I take a deep breath and try to relax. Despite his faults, Ryan is the only family I have left. I'll deal with the money bullshit later—when he's not in the hospital and beat up. "Okay, Amy. I'm going to go to the hospital. I'll call by and check in with you afterward. Get Michael to watch upstairs, and I'll sort everything else out when I come in."

"Right, see you later then," she replies before ending the call.

FUCK!

My mind is spinning as I call my car service and ask for an urgent pick-up before sitting back in my leather chair. With my head in my hands, and my fingers tugging my hair in frustrated concern, I wonder what the fuck Ryan has done this time. I may not know the details yet, but I'm automatically assuming the worst.

I grab my laptop bag, shoving in a few files that need my attention, and walk out the door. As the elevator starts its descent, I'm hit with the reality that my brother is lying in a hospital bed, having been beaten up in my club.

But this isn't the first time something like this has happened.

I was twenty-five and working as a summer associate. I'd been working late one night on a white collar fraud case that had the potential to make my career in corporate law when my cell started ringing. Seeing Ryan's name on the screen, I answered straight away.

"Hey, Ry."

"Sean, I'm in deep shit."

My breath stuttered as his words hit me. "Where are you?"

"Hiding in an alley behind a bar in Detroit."

"Ry, what the fuck? You were in Chicago this morning when I left for work." My voice was restrained as I tried to reel in my growing fury.

"Can we talk about this later? Right now, I need help. I was in the back room when the place was raided. I escaped out the back door and started running. Now, I'm in an alley in downtown Detroit with my phone and twenty bucks to my name." He was breathing hard and his voice was shaky.

My mind was racing. "Fuck, Ry. You seriously need to start sorting your shit out. I can't keep bailing you out. This will seriously fuck up my work on this case."

"I wouldn't call unless I were desperate. I'm stuck, brother." He knew what he was doing.

Our grandfather had died three months earlier, seven months after our grandmother had passed away in her sleep following a long illness. He had never gotten over her death and started withering away right in front of our eyes until the day he'd had a heart attack in the living room. Unfortunately, it was Ryan who came home and found him, and he's struggled ever since. It just exacerbated the problems that started when our parents were killed. Overnight he'd become a thrill seeker; an adrenaline junkie always looking for a rush, wanting to prove to himself that he was still alive.

He decided that he was going to live every day as if it was his last. He lived and loved plentifully. Every woman who caught his eye was a potential soul mate. He loved easily and he loved hard. He also played hard … and often, which is exactly what got him into the trouble in Detroit.

"Ry, I'm a four hour drive away. Even if I tried to get a flight, I wouldn't get there for a few hours."

"Sean, I'm in deep this time. If the cops get wind I was there, I'll go down for this."

"For what?"

"Don't worry about it, it won't happen again. I just need some money or a car or something to get back home."

I remember my stomach tightening and feeling a prickle on my scalp at his sudden evasiveness.

"Shit."

"What, Ryan?" I asked, my voice getting louder and attracting attention from other people around me.

"Bro, track my cell or something. Do whatever you have to do."

"What the fuck, Ryan? What's going on? You're making no sense."

"I'm walking south, two blocks away from the bar."

A moving target. Fucking fantastic. "Ryan, I don't have time for this bullshit."

"Shit," he muttered under his breath, but I heard it clear as day and slid immediately into my default protector mode. The same mode I'd been in for twenty years.

"Ryan, what's the name of the bar?"

"What?"

"The bar where you were …"

He started panting loudly into my ear. "Big Rob's Bar," he replied breathlessly. I heard his footsteps against the pavement loudly echoing down the phone.

"Really, Ry? Big Rob's Bar?"

"Listen, Sean, can you help me?" He sounded desperate.

"Why are you running?"

My jaw was starting to ache from the constant tension. Five minutes of phone conversation and all I'd found out was that he was in Detroit, running from a potential crime scene, and had gone from being worried but relaxed, to being anxious and desperate in a matter of seconds.

I needed a vacation.

"Five of them just crossed the street behind me. Coming up fast. Check the hospitals first," he spat out before I heard yelling in the distance and the phone being dropped. I jumped to my feet, shouting down the phone in desperation. "Ry? Ryan? Fuck! Ryan!"

All I could hear were footsteps and car noise, then Ryan shouting, "No, please! I have nothing. I'm just walking. Shit!" More footsteps, car horns, then what I found out later were three guys laying into my kid brother as he lay in the gutter on the street.

Two of my co-workers had tried to calm me down, but I shook my head at them. I looked at my watch. 1 a.m. "Ryan!" I'd shouted one last time and with no response I made the split second decision to hang up and call 911.

Seven hours later, I landed in Detroit and jumped into a cab which took me straight to the hospital where Ryan was being treated for a concussion and four broken ribs. We returned home the same day via a rental car.

That was the day I discovered my brother had a gambling addiction that led him to a dodgy bar late one night for an illegal back room poker game in which he'd lost five thousand dollars just before the cops arrived.

It was the first of many brushes with the law Ryan Miller was to have, and the first of many bailouts that I'd give him.

Thirty minutes in my town car and I was now in the ER of Northwestern Memorial Hospital trying to find my brother … again. Yes, it's nine years later, but this routine is starting to get old. Even if he was attacked by an alleged robber and is completely innocent in this situation, I'm sick of visiting my kid brother in the fucking hospital. I wait for two hours, which gives me time to boot up my laptop and go through my emails and messages. By the time I'm taken to Ryan, it has been four hours since he was allegedly attacked and I'm told by his nurse that he's very sore and drowsy from the pain meds, so I can't stay long.

I walk into his twin room and see his temporary roommate for the night—an old man who's snoring his head off and drooling on his pillow. To be honest, this man looks like he's in God's waiting room awaiting his call-up. I walk toward the closed curtain beside him and pull it back to see a somewhat battered, younger version of myself lying in the hospital bed in front of me.

His eyes are closed and I can see an impressive bruise forming over his right eye as well as a cut on his cheek. He's wearing what looks like the most unattractive hospital gown I've ever seen, and he's hooked up to a blood pressure/heart monitor which is beeping quietly in the corner. There's an oxygen mask covering his mouth and he's got a wide white bandage wrapped around his head. I chuckle when I get an image of Humpty Dumpty in my head which is exactly who he looks like right now. Then I realize that it's the first time I've laughed in a long time which fucking sucks.

Ryan's eyes open and he stares at me, blinking a few times before a frown mars his face.

"Hey, little brother." I step forward and take a seat in the chair by the bed.

"Hey, big brother," he says, his voice muffled by the mask.

"What's the damage?"

"Physically or financially?"

"Ry, what have—"

"It's bad, Sean. Real bad."

"How bad?"

"Worse than Detroit, bad. Worse than ever before, bad."

You've got to be shitting me. I thought I could come visit him, see he's okay, then go home to a nice glass or two of twenty year old scotch, but no, Ryan has put the kibosh on that plan.

The chair legs scrape against the floor as I stand up and start to pace in the small confined area. My body is rigid, and the anger is rolling off me in waves.

"Sean, they know about you and they know you've got money. Today proves they're gonna try whatever means necessary to—"

"Who are they?"

"I can't tell you that."

I scoff. "Well, fuck. Excuse me while I sit back and let criminals come into my club and try to steal from me, or bash my brother for a fucking gambling debt I didn't know he fucking had. Or wait …" I pause for a moment, bringing my finger to my chin mockingly. "Should I just let them take whatever the FUCK they want from me just to pay YOUR debt? Let them take MY hard earned fucking money just so YOU are in the clear, ONCE AGAIN!" I bellow.

Ryan's eyes go wide at my tirade, but I don't give a fuck. I'm too wound up to care about being gentle with him. I can't pussy foot around this issue. He needs help and he needs it now before he ends up in jail. Or dead.

I glare at him and see his heart rate has gone up slightly. A nurse rushes in with a security guard at her back. "Sir, I must ask that you keep it down or I'll have to ask you to leave. You're upsetting the other patients," she asks in a saccharine sweet voice.

I throw my hands up in the air. "That's fine, I'm done." I look my brother straight in the eyes. "I'm DONE."

I bend down and grab my laptop bag before turning to the nurse who has taken a step back away from me and I stifle a laugh. I've been told before that I can take down a room— or underwear—with a simple look, but this woman looks like she's about to be crushed.

Turning away from Ryan, I step toward the nurse who is watching my every move. I hold my hand out to her. When she tentatively places her hand in mine, I look deep into her eyes, turning on the charm that does me so well in the boardroom and the bedroom. "Please accept my sincere apologies. My brother and I were just having a heated discussion. Can you please have someone call me when my brother is being released? I'll arrange for him to be picked up. He can give you my contact details for payment." And just for added sweetness, I lift her hand to my mouth and kiss it softly. "Have a nice night, ma'am." That earns me a girly giggle. She's way too young for my taste and in no way submissive, so we wouldn't be a good pairing, but a little flirtation never hurt anyone.

I give her and the now scowling security guard a smile and walk out of the room as quickly as possible. I stop across from the door and rest both palms on the wall, my head dropping as I take in everything that just happened. My brother has fucked me over. Not intentionally, of course, but his uncontrollable behavior has brought trouble to my door. I need to think about this and what I can do about it; who I can talk to and how I can pay the debt before anything else happens to my club or staff … or Ryan because Christ only knows I'm a glutton for punishment and I haven't the guts to disown him.

Yet.

Regaining my composure, I push off from the wall and shrug off my jacket. Then pulling at the knot of my tie, I take it off and stuff it in my pocket. Feeling more relaxed, I turn to the elevators and stop dead. Walking toward me is the one woman I never thought I'd see again.

She looks up and falters before she stops in front of me. It's like one of those movie moments where the world around us goes blurry and Sam and I stand there in the middle like we're in a silent showdown.

One that's ten years in the making.

Her emerald green eyes stare into mine, and her sandy-blonde hair flows softly around her face. I'm awestruck. She's even more beautiful than when she was a fresh-faced, radiant woman with the world at her feet at twenty-two.

Samantha Richards, the woman who once held all the power and refused to acknowledge it. The woman who walked out of my life and rejected me with no explanation.

The woman who deserted me at a time when I needed her the most.

CHAPTER 3: "IF YOU EVER COME BACK"

Sam

Time stands still the moment I lock eyes with Sean in the bustling hospital corridor. We stand there staring at each other for what seems like an eternity until my brain finally kicks into gear and I turn to leave.

"Sammy," he says, stopping me in my tracks. I take a deep resigned breath and turn back around to face him—my biggest regret in life.

"Sean. Long time, no see," I say confidently. My mom always told me to tackle each difficult situation with confidence, grace, and a 'take no prisoners' attitude. That advice got me through the police academy and gained me my 'Ice Queen' reputation it seems. Unfortunately, the pensive expression on his face shows he sees right through the façade.

"Are you here visiting?" His eyes drop and I watch as he does a full body scan before returning his stormy-blue gaze back to mine. I struggle to hold back the tremor that surges through me. He still affects me deep to my core.

"Yes, my partner and I were the first on the scene today when Ryan was assaulted," I explain. I'm impressed at my ability to form coherent sentences in front of him, let alone my ability to converse intelligently.

As he lifts his arm and grips the back of his neck, I take the opportunity to look him over. By God, he has aged well. No, scratch that, he has aged fucking well. His dark brown hair is cut short, matching the strong, unyielding personality I knew he once had. When we were together, Sean was a commanding force to be reckoned with. He could always walk into a room and own it within seconds.

When I look at his face again, I'm met with piercing blue eyes that threaten to unnerve me. I square my shoulders, creating an illusion of strength. I can tell that something is troubling him. His chiseled jaw is clenched tight like he's trying to rein in whatever emotion is consuming him.

Just as an uncomfortable silence stretches between us, he quirks an eyebrow at me and his eyes crinkle slightly.

He just caught me checking him out.

C'mon, you can't fault me. I'm a woman nearing the peak of my sexual prime. I haven't had an orgasm in four days, and I'm standing in front of the man who unintentionally ruined me for any other man. Something I'll never admit to him.

Ever.

"You were there first?" he asks incredulously.

"That's what I said," I retort. My defense mechanism emerges from her dreamy Sean trance, stepping into her bitch panties and wearing them with pride.

His gorgeous eyes widen, but he quickly recovers. "Why?"

I know he's assessing me, watching my reactions like a hawk. "I joined the academy after college. Been with Chicago PD ever since." This conversation is as awkward as I knew it would be. Is it ever easy to talk with someone who you can't admit still holds a place deep inside you? A man who you never allowed yourself to have a chance of a future with? Yeah … no!

"I'm getting the impression you're still a hard ass too. At work anyway …" His gaze drops to my mouth, not missing the moment I drag my tongue along my suddenly parched lips. It's a nervous habit that I've never been able to shake, and it's obvious that Sean remembers too because his eyes flare quickly before returning to mine. Putting his hand in his pocket, my attention is drawn to his chest, his hips, his ….

I shake my head and catch the slight curl of his lips into an irresistible smirk. Dammit, he's still the master mind reader he always was. Right, Sam, snap out of it. You're here to check on Ryan then you can go to Helen's and get reacquainted with your friend Vodka.

Hang on.

What did he mean by 'at work anyway'?

"You look well, Sam," he adds, suddenly putting a crack in my armor with a simple compliment. "Had I known you were still in Chicago … well, I would have—"

"I'm just going to pop into Ryan's room and make sure he's okay."

His body jolts and I definitely don't miss the look of disbelief that shadows his expression. He studies my face, unnerving me to the core. "Do you have plans tonight?" His confidence is unmistakable as he waits for my answer.

An unexpected wave of warmth spread through my body from the fact that he wants to see me again. He's gotten to me, just from a simple five minute conversation. I feel like I'm against the ropes with little to no options of winning. My eyes widen as I look at his lips again. "Yes." My voice shakes slightly and the slowly growing smile on his lips tells me he didn't miss it. "I'm going to my friends' place for dinner." I look down at my watch and realize that visiting hours will be over soon. "Sorry, Sean, but I'd better get to Ryan before visiting hours end. Great to see you again though," I lie through my teeth. It's fucking terrifying and thrilling at the same time.

He steps back, not appearing rattled or shocked by my act. "I see," he murmurs. "Well, thanks for helping Ryan this afternoon. I know it's your job, but he was knocked around a bit and it must have made him feel better knowing you were there. I own that club, so if there is anything you need … professionally, or any questions that need answers, please don't hesitate." He's all business now as he pulls out his business card and hands it to me. I look at him and then the card before taking it in my fingertips. When my hands brush against his, the energy between us is palpable.

I adjust my purse on my shoulder and stand straight, almost eye to eye with this foreboding and gorgeous man from my past. In a split second that gives me no hope of evasion, he takes a step forward and wraps his arm around my waist, resting his hand on the small of my back and bringing my body close to his. Kissing my cheek, he brings his mouth so close to my ear that I tingle with the sensation of his warm breath on my skin.

"Until next time, Sammy ..." He kisses a spot just below my ear, turning the tingle into a full body shiver of the good but embarrassingly obvious kind, before he steps away, pulling his arm away and walking down the corridor away from me.

I stand there dumbstruck, replaying the whole scene that just played out between us.

Then it hits me.

He can tell.

With one look, a few exchanged words and a brief physical interaction, he can tell.

Fuck a duck and stuff me with a feather. I never could fool him, not with a simple fib or a lie by omission. He always knew. Right from the beginning he'd told me that he loved my backbone and sass but when it was just the two of us behind closed doors, I was his. Now, the one thing I couldn't admit to myself back then, the part of me he wanted to nurture, just revealed itself to Sean in all its glory.

But that's in my past, and I realized a long time ago that as hard as you try, you can't change what has gone before. You can only learn from it. And this time, Sean's the one walking away from me, not the other way around.

Irony sucks ass sometimes.

I take a deep breath and walk down the corridor to the nurses' station, asking directions toward Ryan's room. When I find him, he's staring out the window looking lost. His vacant stare and downturned mouth seem unnatural on his face. This is Ryan, the guy who always used to liven up the mood of any room he walked into. He's the happy go lucky to Sean's intense and broody. The combination always made for a good time. But looking at the man lying in the hospital bed in front of me, all I can see is a lone man who looks like he's lost everything.

"Ryan?" I say hesitantly. He slowly turns his head toward me and his body goes rigid in surprise, then relaxes again, although the wince I see cannot be missed. "How are you feeling?" My voice is still soft. I've had a lot of practice dealing with victims of crime, but something tells me that this is something else, something important that I've missed.

He shrugs his shoulders and turns his head back to the window. "Did you see my brother?" he asks, his voice flat and without feeling.

"Yeah, I did. Not my favorite thing in the world I must admit."

"Why's that? You two haven't seen each other in what … ten years?" He still won't look away from the window.

I sit down on the bed beside his legs and gently put my hand on top of the blanket to get his attention. "Ry, did something happen? With Sean?"

He slowly turns his head and stares at me as if I have two heads. His right eye is almost swollen shut and he has a bandage around his head covering his wound. He studies me for what seems like forever before he asks, "Are you here as a friend or as a cop, Sam? Because the answer to that will determine my answer to your question."

My eyes widen in surprise. I've never been asked that before so I've never had to consider it. But Ryan was my friend, Sean's brother, and right now, I'm guessing he needs a friend. I shake my head. "As your friend, Ryan. Please tell me what's going on so I can help you."

He gives me the slightest of nods before taking a slow, measured breath. "Sean basically washed his hands of me just before you arrived."

I gasp. No, that can't be right. The two of them are the only family they have left. "No …"

He lets out a laugh then gasps in pain. "Shit, that hurts. Yep, my brother has finally had enough of my shit. He's sick of being the father, the brother and the fixer-upper." He looks back out the window and I know I'm losing him again.

"Ryan, Sean loves you. You guys used to be so close and you're working at the club. He wouldn't just walk away."

He jerks his head back to me. "Did you not see him walk away a few minutes ago? God! He was yelling so loud that the nurse had to call security. Your precious Sean has decided he's done and what he says goes, so he's leaving me to deal with my own shit and I don't blame him. I'm in a lot of debt, and I think that's what today at the club was all about. Robbery gone bad is what it looks like but that guy was there to rough me up and send a message. Well, message fucking received."

He takes a breath again, then sighs loudly. "Maybe you should go, Sammy. You seem to like leaving when the going gets tough. Oh wait, nope. You just leave when someone dies and we need you."

I swallow to try and rid myself of the large lump that's made itself home in my throat. Fuck! No wonder Sean looked at me with a wariness that I'd never seen on him before. Although, there's probably a lot of anger there too. It was a long time ago, but my departure from their lives was sudden and came as a shock. I had to cut all ties for my own heart. But that's a story for another time.

"Ry, I didn't mean for it to happen like that. I'm sorry. One day I might tell you about it, but in all honesty, that's between Sean and me."

His eyes follow me as I get off the bed and stand up. "Sorry, it's none of my business. Please …"

I'm suddenly taken back to Ryan as the impressionable seventeen year old boy I met all those years ago.

"I've got to get going, Ry." I reach into my pocket and pull out a business card. "But here's my card. If you need me, you call. Maybe I can help with Sean. I don't know if he'd be receptive to talking with me, but if you want me to I'll try."

Seeing Sean again must have fried my damn brain. I'm volunteering to act as a go-between for the Miller brothers. Wonders will never cease.

Or maybe, subconsciously, I just want to see Sean again.

Vodka. I need vodka, stat!.

CHAPTER 4 – "DRINK YOU AWAY"

Sam

"More vodddkaaaa," I mumble into my glass as I down my fifth drink. How did I get here?

As I was leaving the hospital, I sent Helen a text telling her I needed a drink—or ten!—and that I was on my way. See, that's what is so great about having a best friend who is exactly like you. A simple text of 'I need Vodka stat. Just saw Sean' tells her everything she needs to know and why.

On my way to her place, I couldn't get Sean and our not entirely unexpected but still surprising conversation out of my head.

Sean was always able to elicit a reaction from me. Whether it was riling me up, shocking me, or more often than not, turning me on with a single heated look. I could never read him though. He was always unexpected, but positively so. Despite his tragic family loss at such a young age, he was strong and in control. He had dreams and aspirations, and he saw what he wanted and went after it without hesitation.

And the day we met, what he wanted and went after was me.

It was our junior year in college. We were two pre-law students sitting on opposite sides of the auditorium and squaring off during a political science class. The impromptu debate over the effectiveness of the modern Republican idealism was thrilling, infuriating and heated. Sean's cocky smirk and laid back demeanor was evident as he traded barbs and opinions back and forth with me. In the end, the professor had to get us to agree to disagree, but even from across the room, our chemistry was undeniable.

When the end of class came, I was still riled up, the adrenaline from the exchange coursing through me, so I was too distracted to notice him come up next to me. When I stood up with my bag and leaned forward, I caught the underside of his chin with my head on the way up.

"Fucking hell, woman, no need to hurt me." I regained my balance and stood back, looking up into the most captivating blue eyes I had ever seen. Close up, Sean's face was all male; angular with a strong jaw, and the most kissable lips I'd ever seen. I lost myself in his gaze, but I didn't miss the curling of his lips.

He held out his hand for me to shake. "I don't believe we've met. I'm Sean Miller, the stubborn and argumentative man who had the pleasure of arguing with you today." His grin got impossibly bigger as I stood there, equally taken aback and turned on by his candid approach.

Looking down at his hand, I shook my head to clear the hot guy fog that was threatening to take over, and put my hand in his, gripping firmly. My mother's words of appearing strong and unwavering echoed through my mind. "Sam, Sam Richards. Pleased to meet another steadfast student." I pulled my hand away when the heat radiating from his tall, foreboding body started to get to me. "Sorry, but I have to get to my next class."

He took a step back to let me pass, but caught me by the elbow and stepped forward into my personal space, his mouth ending up mere inches from my face. "Dinner, drinks, movie, coffee … you name it I'm there, Sam."

I righted myself and turned my head to face him, a shudder wracking my body as his breath fanned over my face. Yes, he was that close. "You'll have to try harder than that. A good smile and confident swagger will not get this warm body in your bed. If you really want to know me, Sean, you'll find a way to get my attention."

Then I walked away.

It didn't take long for him to get my attention. It took a little longer to get me into his bed, but that's a whole other story.

———————————————————————

I was met at Helen's apartment door twenty minutes later with a smile and a freshly poured dose of sedation disguised as a vodka tonic.

"What did he do?" she asks, shutting the door behind me.

"Nothing," I reply two gulps later as I walk to the kitchen where I spot a nearly full bottle of Grey Goose waiting for me.

"I call bullshit," she states matter-of-factly.

"Where's Rico?" I pour my second glass with a very healthy ratio of liquor to mixer.

"Gone for a run. Stop changing the subject, Sam." She puts her hands on her hips and looks at me expectantly.

I ignore her and down my second drink just as quickly as the first before I continue. "Thank god! That gives me time to get a few drinks under my belt before he dishes out his manly wisdom."

She smirks. "Well, someone's got to talk you down off the ledge. You keep up that pace and you'll be legless in half an hour."

"One can only hope," I mumble.

"Hon, pour a fresh one and come sit down. At least slow down to a slow jog rather than a sprint."

I sigh loudly. "Oh, all right then. God, when did I suddenly give a shit about him again?"

She picks her wine glass up off the kitchen counter. "Potty mouth Sam is in the house, so it must be bad. At least my night will be entertaining if nothing else." I scowl at her back before following her into the living room with the vodka and tonic bottles, then plop myself down on her large, gray, suede sectional that is even more comfortable than it looks. I turn and rub my face against the back of the couch.

"I think I want to marry your sectional," I say with a sigh.

"Holy shit, woman, how much vodka did you put in those drinks? You're talking about making a commitment with an inanimate piece of furniture. This must be bad."

"The worst. No ... the best. No, wait. Oh, fuck. I dunno. He's Sean fucking Miller. Love of my life, regret of the century. The superstar of my fantasies." I look her straight in the eye and I'm immediately cut to the quick by the sincerity and concern I see reflected on her face. "I'm screwed aren't I?"

"Oh, believe me, I can tell you're going to be if that man is still as potent and panty-dropping good as he used to be. Sammy, you need to take control of the situation. I remember how much of a mess you were last time, but you've grown now. You have your own mind and you know what and who you are now. Why is this affecting you so much?" She looks at my glass, then back at my face.

Leaning forward, I pour drink number four into my glass on the coffee table, take a long sip, then bury myself back into the future sofa of my dreams.

"He's aged so damn well, Hels. Seriously, he was hot in college, smoking hot. The good boy with an edge. But now ... now he looks wiser, more dignified. And by God, the way he looked at me? It was like he could see right through my armor and was studying my soul."

"So what's the problem then?"

"He's strong, irresistible and likes to dominate."

"This isn't anything new, hon. And a long time ago, he really used to do it for ya."

I try to boost my flailing confidence by taking another drink. "Okay, so you know the club you picked up his brother from today?"

"Uh, yeah, everyone under thirty-five in Chicago knows about Throb."

"Did you know about upstairs?"

"The question is how do YOU know about upstairs?"

"Oh, c'mon, Hels. I'm a cop, word spreads. But it was Zander who told me actually. There are private rooms up there for," I lift my spare hand and do an air quote, "stuff." With that, Helen bursts out laughing—a bent in half, 'have to put the wine glass down and hug herself' laugh.

Rico walks in, panting and out of breath, and looking every inch the hot Brazilian man he is. He looks at me and smiles. "Hey, Sammy." Then he sees Helen laughing her ass off and tilts his head sideways, still standing by the now closed front door. "Minha vida, what on earth is so funny?" he asks with a smile on his face as he takes a few large steps to the couch and leans over the back of it to lay a big fat one on Helen's smiling lips.

I look over at them and sigh loudly and happily. "That's a new one. What does that mean?"

Rico looks over at me then back to Helen, his eyes full of love and adoration for his wife to be. "It means my life."

Oh my God. I want that! "Guys, you're making me all jealous and swoony. Please resume normal programming and let me wallow with my bedmate for a while," I say, holding up the bottle of vodka.

Rico circles the couch and sits between us, not caring that he's covered in sweat. He wraps an arm around my shoulder and pulls me to his side. "What's wrong, Sammy? Whose ass do I need to go kick?"

"Mine," I mumble.

"Never gonna happen. Try again," he adds with an encouraging squeeze.

"No, hang on." Helen recovers from her laughing fit and turns to me. "Sam, I love you to death and always will, but you're no prude. I know that and you know that. So why does … oh, hell. Why does the 'stuff' make you uneasy?"

I open my mouth to reply but stop and look down at the empty glass in my hands instead. Does it make me uneasy? Or is it simply a case of the guilt bestowed upon me from the past? Shit! I look up at Helen and Rico who are both waiting for my answer.

"Fuck!" I say loudly. "You know what, Hels, you're right. But Sean is in a whole world above that. One look down a hospital corridor and I was mush. I mean, melted into a puddle on the floor. He looked angry and annoyed and intense, then he saw me and that look turned to shock." My drunken verbal diarrhea stage has begun it seems.

"You need to see him again," Rico states directly. "You two have always had unfinished business, Sam. You broke up and then you went MIA from his life. You told me it was hard for you. Well, newsflash, honey. If he were as into you as you were into him, he would have felt it just as much as you did. Us macho men may seem tough, but we feel too, you know."

"What about Tanner?" Helen pipes up.

I narrow my eyes, confused as to what the hell my not-so-much-a-friend-with-really-good-benefits has to do with this. "What about him?"

"Does he get you all wound up like this?"

"No! Fuck no!"

Rico clears his throat and I jerk my eyes to him to see him giving me an all-knowing smile. I let my head fall back onto the couch and I groan, taking in Rico's words of male wisdom. "Rico, do you always have to make so much fucking sense?"

"I see Sam's dirty mouth is with us. Exactly how much has she had to drink?" he asks Helen, who starts laughing her ass off again, which starts me off. Soon enough, we're all laughing.

Well, at least they took my mind off him I suppose.

CHAPTER 5 – "TAKE ME OR LEAVE ME"

Sean

After leaving the hospital, I went to the club to check on things. Amy had everything under control, so once I'd made all the necessary arrangements to cover Ryan's absence, I called for a car and headed home to my condo.

Dropping my keys on the hall table, I turn the lights on before walking up the stairs and into the living room. I pour myself a drink and walk to the front windows, leaning against them as I watch the city lights dance in front of me. The hustle and bustle of the city below calms me somehow. Even though I'm not from Chicago, this city has become my home and has held my heart for twenty-one years now. The Bears, The Cubs, The Bulls, Lake Michigan, Cloud Gate, Wicker Park, the South Loop, Michigan Avenue … the list goes on.

I bought my condo in the middle of the city. The brick and stone exterior sold me at first, then the polished wood floors of the living area, the mezzanine floor bedroom that I now call my own, and the rooftop that opens up to the surrounding skyscrapers. It's bold and strong, yet welcoming with an inner warmth—a sanctuary in the middle of the busy metropolis. A perfect representation of me, and one day I hope to have a wife and family here too. I mean, I am thirty-three. I suppose it's time to start thinking about things like that.

I smile to myself briefly before the day's events creep back into the forefront of my mind. Ryan's epic fuck up, and Sammy. Samantha Richards.

The unexpected blast from the past that has rocked me to the core.

How can she still get under my skin after all these years? Ten years is a long time for me to hold a candle. Actually a candle is too tame, too timid to describe the myriad of feelings I have for Sammy. A raging inferno or thermonuclear blast would be more apt. It had always been like that with us.

Back when we first met, I thought she was someone who understood me, accepted me, someone I could take care of and who matched me yin for yang both in and out of the bedroom. Then her harsh rejection of our relationship—of me—doused any flame between us.

Let's be honest, I haven't exactly lead a life of chastity since she left me. The break up affected me more than I'd care to admit, so I buried myself in school and women. It's always been the same. If I see something that interests me, someone that catches my interest, I go after it (or them) because a long time ago I learned that you can't bank on anything.

I make sure that the women I'm with are willing, fully aware that it's a one-time deal, casual at best, and more than capable of giving me the power exchange I seek.

I've always known that I was dominant. Yes, I was a big brother who was forced to grow up quickly when my parents died, but it was more than that. When I first met Sammy, she was feisty and sassy. She gave as good as she got and that grabbed my attention. When I asked her out she declined, but offered me a challenge to capture her attention in other ways.

In the early days with Sam, I hid my controlling ways. I finally got her to say yes to a date with me after three weeks and a large bouquet of flowers delivered to her apartment every day for a week. When we started sleeping together, I slowly showed my true nature to her. At first she was hesitant, but as we traveled down the path of the mutually beneficial power exchange in the bedroom, and all the pleasures I could show her, she bloomed. She was happier, freer, and if anything she became stronger out of the bedroom, and it just made me love her even more.

But by the end, it didn't matter anyway.

I always suspected she was a natural submissive. The beauty was that she didn't know. It was just second nature to her. We clicked instantly because of that. Our chemistry was like dynamite. Whatever the real reason she broke up with me, whatever the lies she told me to make herself believe she was making the right decision, that was never in question.

To me, sex is a beautiful act that should be enjoyed. The act of submission, having a beautiful woman willingly submit to me, is one of the greatest gifts. I'm a dominant. I like to dominate women during sex. I own it. I don't hide it, and I've never tried to. There is nothing depraved or wrong with it, and there are a number of women equally submissive who get off on being controlled.

I don't get into all the high protocol BDSM shit. For me, there is no need for presenting poses, contracts, or discussions about soft or hard limits. That's not to say I don't enjoy giving a damn good erotic spanking when the moment presents itself.

The club has a safe word that is used by everyone. There are viewing holes on the doors of every VIP room so the VIP Duty Manager can check on everything and everyone at any time. This is one of the important parts of the contract signed by our key holders. However, it's their responsibility to negotiate with their partners before entering their room.

Four years ago, I found myself in a position to expand my investment portfolio. I came across a nightclub in a precarious financial situation and the moment I walked into the large two-story brick and mortar building I knew I'd found what I was looking for.

Throb. My home away from home.

Having been a long time member of a few clubs in my time, I decided to mix business with pleasure—my own nightclub with private VIP rooms upstairs for exclusive use. The notoriety of those VIP rooms was enough to bring in the crowds, and for almost two years now, Throb has been one of the hippest and hottest Chicago clubs. It's the club to see and be seen at.

Other than my condo, it's the one place where I can be my true self. Where there are no restrictions, no judgment. To be honest, if people want to judge me and the club's illicit reputation, then they shouldn't have even stepped through the black marble doors. It's that very reputation that brings people in.

Throb is also the only place where I play. I made sure that I had a personal VIP room for my exclusive use. And although I say I never take on regular subs, there was one woman who was my exception. Makenna Lewis. But that girl is every man's exception. She was always straight up and to the point, walking to the beat of her own drum. She had different needs, and three 'friends' who tended to those needs. We all knew the deal, and according to Mac, we were all okay with it.

As we reached the door to my private VIP room, I turned around, pulling her so that her back was flush with the door and proceeded to take her mouth with reckless abandon. She gasped at my ferocity, allowing my probing tongue welcome access into her mouth. I remember groaning at the taste of her—tequila and lemon. I wanted to devour her.

I continued to taunt her, using the kiss as a promise to claim her body as my own just for that one night. I eased back from the kiss, lightly scraping my teeth along her lower lip, eliciting a shudder from Mac that I felt travel through her entire body.

"Tonight, baby doll, you're mine. Do you understand that?"

She nodded, seemingly speechless. Her breathing was labored, causing my already hammering cock to harden impossibly further. I was turned on by the power she was letting me have over her, her willingness to give herself and her body over to me, and I planned to show her everything I had to give, to consume her, bring her to new heights she'd never fantasized about.

Even with just a few words spoken between us, I knew Mac was different. She wasn't the type to get clingy, but she wasn't indifferent either. She struck me as a woman who knew what she wanted and what she needed, and unlike Sam, she knew how to get it.

I couldn't take my eyes off her. From the moment I'd seen her across the club, I knew that I'd have her tonight. With my hand firmly gripping her hip, and the other braced on the wall beside her head, I caged her in, bringing my body in close to hers without touching. I focused on the heat raging between us, the unspoken promise of a night full of passion and satisfaction. This moment was partly to make it known that she was safe with me, but also to keep her off balance.

Moving my hand from the door, I pulled out my gold VIP key from my pocket and unlocked the door behind me. Wrapping my arm around her back, I eased the door open, guiding her body backwards into the room while slamming my mouth down onto hers. This time she met me stroke for stroke. We both lost ourselves in the kiss—sensual, erotic, and hot as fucking hell.

A growl rumbled in my chest as she tightened her grip in my hair, fisting the strands as if her life depended on it and I was her anchor. My lust soared and before I knew it the door was slammed shut behind us and her back was flat against it as I devoured every inch of exposed skin—her neck, her collarbone, that delightful spot below a woman's ear that has them trembling every single time.

Mustering all the self-control I had, I ripped my mouth away from her, nipping a trail along her jaw before reaching her ear, deciding it was time to tell her exactly what I had planned for our time together. "You're so fucking hot, baby doll. I can't wait to have your ass warm from my hand. To have you laid out before me, begging to be fucked."

I trailed my tongue down her neck, sinking my teeth into the delicate skin of her neck. There was something about Mac that pushed all my Dom buttons. The moment that I felt her body melt into mine, submitting to me, I soared. I murmured my appreciation of her body, promising to make her come hard, multiple times, promises I had every intention of following through on. I slipped my fingers between the mesh fabric of her dress, sweeping it slowly down her shoulder, drawing out the experience for both of us, exposing the expanse of her creamy skin to my hungry gaze. I followed suit with the other shoulder until the dress pooled at her feet, following the trail of the material with soft nips and open mouth kisses down her arm and back up again until I could use my tongue to trace a wet line across the curve of her surging breasts. Drawing out this part of a scene always amped up the anticipation for both of us, and Mac was as much about anticipation and delayed gratification as I was. At this stage she was gasping, her breaths coming out in short pants. It was fucking sexy to see a woman so responsive to my touch, my mouth, and it only bode well for the moment I sunk my cock eight inches deep inside of her.

"Hands on the door. Don't move," I commanded as I dragged my hands up to cradle her bare breasts, swiping my thumbs across her straining nipples through the silky material covering them. Mac's raspy moan echoed around the room like erotic music to my ears. "Fucking beautiful, baby doll," I murmured low and deep, hooking my fingers inside the corset and roughly pulling it down, exposing her naked breasts to my feasting eyes. With a lack of control I could not rationalize at the time, I dipped my mouth to taste her skin before sucking the straining peaks deeply into my mouth, raking my teeth gently against the sensitive skin.

Arching her back into my hands and mouth, I pressed her hard nub firmly between my tongue and the roof of my mouth, increasing the pressure until I heard a gratifying moan. I pulled away, moving a few steps back and staring at her, my eyes half open and full of heat as I took the opportunity to take her in.

"We need to get these clothes off," I spat out before grabbing her dress gathered at her waist and tugging it down her legs until she was left standing half naked in front of me. My mouth watered. Left in nothing but the sexiest corset I'd ever seen and strappy black heels, she was just as exquisite as I knew she'd be.

Then as luck would have it, my night got even better when she lost her head and pulled her hands off the door, forgetting my command to leave them there. Wrapping her arms around my shoulders, she pulled her body tight against mine. Unable to resist, I buried my mouth in her neck and trailed one hand down the side of her body, gliding past her hip before finding my target, the warm soaking wet crevice between her legs.

"Oh, baby doll, you're so wet for me. Such a shame that you disobeyed," I said, my voice low and menacing. "My hand is going to warm your ass until you're begging me to be inside you." She moaned encouragingly and I had to reel the desire to busy myself deep inside her then and there.

Not leaving her any time to absorb what I'd just promised to do to her, I grabbed her hand and led her over to the black leather, one-seater chair. I sat down, leaving her standing naked before me. My cock was pulsing hard against my slacks and I didn't miss Mac licking her lips at the sight. As her eyes traveled down my body, I cleared my throat, causing her eyes to snap back to mine. I couldn't hold back a grin; my effect on her was written all over her face. She wanted this just as much if not more than I did, and fuck, if that wasn't the sexiest thing I'd seen in a long time.

"Now would be the time to change your mind, Mac. Otherwise, in less than thirty seconds I'm going to have your bare ass lying across my lap, and my hand stinging from the hard spanking I intend to give you," I stated, quirking my brow in an unspoken challenge.

What happened after that proved to me that Mac was every bit the submissive I'd hoped she'd be. She acquiesced beautifully, the giving over of her body and mind to me all the more gratifying. It was a gift that I honored every time we were together in the twelve months following.

She reminds me a lot of my Sammy actually. When Mac and I were together, she bloomed under my strong hand and commanding nature. She told me once that it was one of the most powerful releases she had ever had, and she relished the freedom she felt by walking into my private room at the club and leaving all decisions at the door. The only decision she had to make was putting her hand in mine the first night we met. Something she did willingly. It was sexy as hell.

What made me more proud was when Makenna called me over to her house to let me know that she had finally let herself fall for a man, something she had previously never allowed herself to do. Our relationship was never about a long term commitment. There were no feelings beyond friendship and healthy sexual chemistry.

But now, seeing my Sammy has me contemplating taking my own advice, the same guidance I gave Makenna eight months ago.

"Whatever happened in the past belongs in the past. Learn from it, grow, and move on. Don't let it determine your future."

If my parents' deaths taught me anything, it was that life can change on the turn of a dime so you have to live it like it could be your last day on earth.

If only it were that easy.

CHAPTER 6 – "PLAYING WITH MY HEART"

Sam

I've had two glorious days off work after a six shift stint. Two days that included me sleeping off a rather large hangover in Helen and Rico's guest room for half a day, then the other half of yesterday was spent having a mental health day on my couch watching television cop dramas. Yeah, I know. Don't ask!

Now, it's my second day off, my last before I return to work, and wouldn't you know it, I can't sleep in for the life of me. It's 10 a.m. and I've been up for a few hours. First, I put on my running gear and go to work out in Lincoln Park. Then I grab a cleansing smoothie from my favorite café and get home thirty minutes later, planting myself on the wooden stool at my kitchen counter to read the newspaper. I know I can read it online, and a lot of people probably do, but there is something about the smell of a broadsheet newspaper … the smudging of the newsprint on your fingers, the folding of page after page giving you that indescribable smell that's full of memories, moments in time you'll never forget.

From my place in my small kitchen, I start hearing a weird vibrating type noise coming from my bedroom. I have a moment of sheer horror flash before my eyes then I remember that:

a) I live alone.

b) I'm a thirty-two year old woman, so who the fuck cares that I have three vibrators, one vibrating egg, and a vibrating pair of underwear that Helen bought me on a dare.

c) I didn't use my sex toy collection last night because I fell asleep on the couch in the middle of Castle.

d) The noise is not going away by me sitting here considering all the different vibrating toys I have in my top right drawer.

Right …

I jump up and run into my bedroom just as the noise stops. What the fuck! Now I'll never know. I scan my room for anything suspicious and come up empty.

Then the noise starts again. I drop to my hands and knees, crawling around looking for the source of the ghost vibration, and giggling because now I'm wondering what happens to sex toys after they die.

Helen would have a field day with this conversation.

I realize the sound is coming from my bed, so pulling back the comforter to an empty bed, I lift my pillows to find my phone vibrating like a kid at Christmas. I lunge for the phone and roll over onto my back at the same time, feeling pretty good about my ability to answer the call and do a side roll at the same time.

"Hello?"

"Sam, is that you?" I hear a deep male voice rumble down the phone. My heart stutters for a minute before he continues. "It's Ryan. Sorry, did I disturb you? I called before, but there was no answer."

I let out the breath I was holding. Why was I suddenly hoping it was Sean? Why would Sean ring me anyway?

Oh shit, Ryan's waiting. "Hey, Ryan, sorry, how are you feeling?"

"I'm a little better."

"That's great, Ry. Glad to hear it," I reply, not hiding my happiness at his recovery. He definitely had me worried last time I saw him at the hospital. Unfortunately, it wasn't his physical recovery I was most worried about.

"Yeah. Hey, listen … I'm at the hospital and they're discharging me today. I need a favor."

A lot of thoughts rush through my head. What if he wants me to look after him? Or needs me to do something illegal? Would he ask me to do something illegal? It's bad enough that he told me in very vague terms that the break in at the club was most likely just something made to look like a robbery. What's done is done though, and if I have information pertaining to a crime that may or may not have taken place, as an officer of the law it's my duty to pass that information on. Which is exactly what I'll do in the morning when I go and speak to the detectives investigating the case.

"You still there, Sammy?" he asks when I go silent.

"Yeah, Ry, just waiting to hear what you need."

"I hate to ask but …" he hesitates, making me more anxious. I don't realize that I'm gripping the phone tightly until the plastic exterior starts digging into my skin. "Um, are you able to give me a ride from the hospital? I, uh, I can't ring Sean and I, uh, haven't got my wallet or keys on me because everything was at the club when I got brought in."

Oh, thank you, Lord!

"Oh sure, Ryan. Of course. What time do you need me?"

"An hour? Is that okay?"

"Absolutely. I'll see you in the waiting room in about an hour then?"

His voice loses its tightness and he's back to sounding relaxed and worry-free (for the moment anyway). "Thanks, Sammy. I knew I could count on you."

"See you soon, Ry." I end the call and drop my phone onto my pillow beside me. Am I living in some alternate dimension all of a sudden?

Is this like Lost Season six where there is a parallel universe and there are really two Sams? Because if there are and she's in the past … god, there is some advice I'd like to give Alternate Sam on her future and the decisions

47

she's due to make.

For our first date, Sean had told me to wear something comfortable. It was a Saturday lunch date and he'd told me nothing about his plans, so I'd dressed in a pair of tight, black, hip-hugging jeans and a white graphic tee that I'd picked up from a vintage store a few weeks earlier. I finished off the look with a rainbow colored scarf draped once around my neck with the ends hanging down. Hey, cut me some slack, it was 2003 you know!

Sean arrived a few minutes early, knocking on my dorm room door just before lunch. When I opened the door to greet him, I had to take a few moments to catch my breath. He'd gelled his hair into a sexy as hell faux hawk and had paired a crisp green polo shirt with a pair of loose fitting khaki pants. Think Justin Timberlake in his early solo days and you'd be right on the money. Suddenly I wasn't feeling nervous about the date, but I was keen to race out the door before my best friend and roommate Helen could see him and start drooling. And to be honest, I wanted to be seen in public with the man who looked like sex on legs.

You see, having been avidly pursued by Sean for the weeks beforehand, I was excited about the date. In fact, I'd been a bouncing hot mess of anticipation all week. Helen was about ready to lace my water with downers just to get me off my high. But nothing was bringing me down, not even a call from my mother wondering why I'd only gotten an A- on a term paper could dull my shine.

"Bye, Helen," I called out to her from the doorway.

"Hey, slapper, wait a minute. I want to check out that fine piece of … oh, shit! Hi." Her face turned a hilarious shade of bright red as she rounded the door to come face to face with a now grinning Sean Miller.

"Hi. Helen is it?" he said, holding out his hand to hers. Even at twenty-two, Sean was all about manners and treating others right. It was the old fashioned values that his grandparents had instilled in him, following the foundation built by his parents before they died.

"Y-Yes. Hi. Sorry, I suffer from a debilitating condition called verbal vomit. Don't hold it against me. Well, unless you want to …"

I whacked her arm and laughed. "Helen!" I chastised but couldn't stop laughing. "Sorry, Sean, let's get out of here before her condition worsens."

"Bye. Have fun, children. Don't rush home." She smiled a shit eating grin, all the while waggling her eyebrows at me before I scoffed and shut the door behind us.

When we reached street level, Sean grabbed my hand and entwined his fingers in mine. Such a simple, straightforward, everyday gesture but it got the butterflies in my stomach excited all over again.

"Do you mind walking for a bit?" he asked assuredly. There was one thing that Sean never showed the world, and that was uncertainty. He was always so black and white, yes or no, left or right. It was one of the things that made me give in to this date. He was stubborn and tenacious like a dog with a bone. He wouldn't let up until I relented and agreed to a date.

We walked for about ten minutes, stopping outside Shedd Aquarium. "Oh, wow. Is this where we're going?" I asked excitedly.

He chuckled and pulled my hand, drawing my body in close to his. "I wanted to wow you with a first date you'd never forget. First stop, the aquarium," he replied with a smile.

"This is awesome. I've never been." I couldn't stop grinning as we walked inside, Sean paid for our tickets and we spent the next two hours exploring the stunning sea creatures and exhibits.

By the time we walked out, it was nearing 3 p.m. and my stomach was growling loudly. Embarrassing! Thankfully Sean was one step ahead of me, leading me into a Mexican restaurant nearby.

"I hope you like some heat," he murmured suggestively as he pulled out a chair for me.

"Well, how hot can you handle it, Sean?"

Pushing in my chair, he bent down low until his breath fanned over my ear. "I want it as hot as you can give me." I clenched my thighs as my breathing became stuttered and the room turned into an inferno.

Thankfully, a waiter interrupted our verbal foreplay, but the seed had been planted.

When he walked me to my door a while later, I was reluctant to end our date. The conversation flowed effortlessly, the sparks between us were strong and addictive, and every time I looked at the man I wanted to jump his bones.

Standing at my door, I turned around. "Thank you for this afternoon. I had an awesome day with you."

Lifting our still joined hands, he pulled me toward his body, wrapping his other arm around my back and holding me close against him. Gasping in shock, his eyes bored into mine, piercing me in place with such passion that I was speechless. When his gaze dropped to my mouth, I was done for. No one else mattered at that moment. It was just Sean and I standing outside my door, about to kiss for the first time.

As he tilted his chin down and softly started to kiss me, I knew that there was no way in hell I would be able to say no to this man again.

I jump up off the bed, pulling my clothes off as I head into my bathroom. I turn the rainfall shower head on, one of the first things I installed when I bought my apartment, and do my daily ritual in the mirror:

1) Check for any new gray hairs. (sigh)

2) Make sure I'm not following the path of my grandmother with stray

lip and chin whiskers (definitely not a family tradition I wish to follow).

When the glass fogs and the room fills with steam, I step into the shower. As I wash myself with my coconut body scrub, my mind wanders back to a time when Sean was my conductor and I was nothing but a violin in his orchestra. He'd been more than upfront with me from the beginning about his dominating ways when it came to sex. I wasn't too surprised to be honest. It was something about the way he carried himself, the way he spoke, his voice and how it felt like it could reach inside you and play you like a puppet. We complimented each other beautifully but no more so than during sex. The man could light my body on fire like no one else. In fact, no one since has made me feel anything even closely resembling the intense passion that pulsed between us.

Without realizing it, my soapy hands had wandered, becoming acutely aware of my throbbing lady garden …

Yes, I said lady garden. Isn't it sexy?

Have you ever wondered what you'd call your vagina if you had a choice? Would you call it a name like Gretel or Elizabeth? Or would you give it a term of endearment like petal or sweetheart? Do you think like a man and call it a c*nt or a pussy? Or are you like me who had a somewhat conservative upbringing with a controlling Army mom who wouldn't hear of anything other than 'lady parts' and 'man parts'. Yes, you read that right. 'Never let a stranger tend to your garden, Samantha' she'd say to me. Looking back, it's a wonder that I ever got laid.

Subconsciously, my fingers stroke over my sensitized skin as I remember all that was good about my Sean of a decade ago. The way he'd let his stubble grow a day too long and how he knew how much I loved the rasp of the coarse hair against my skin as he worked his way down my body, drawing out shudders of pleasure as I relished in the friction, the way he demanded my attention the whole time he would go down on me, how we'd lock eyes as he dove his tongue-deep inside me, how he'd make me so crazy with desire I'd scream down the walls as I rode out my climax, usually multiple times. It's when I remember those bright blue eyes boring into me, willing me to come, that the flashback is too much and my body pulses with the waves of my orgasm as it crashes over me. God damn! Even in my mind Sean is just as good as he always was. I think my fortified willpower when it comes to strong, domineering men might be under attack. I make a mental note to ring Tanner and arrange to meet up with him one night this week.

Once I'm dressed and ready to leave, I google Sean's offices on my phone and pull up his number before pushing send and walking out my door to my parking garage.

"Sean Miller's office. How may I assist you?" an uppity voice answers.

"Hi, I need to speak to Sean," I say quickly, sounding slightly more irritated that I want to be, but me and uppity don't work well together. Miss Bouncy Bones (new name) replies, "Sorry, but Mr. Miller is working from home today. Can I take a message to give him tomorrow?"

"No, that's okay. It's Sam Richards from CPD. Just wanted to check in after the break in the other day. No doubt one of the detectives on the case will contact Mr. Miller once they've concluded their investigation. Thanks though." I hang up the phone so damn fast that her ear might have gotten whiplash.

Fuck! I check my watch and see that I'm running late after the extended shower session. I put my car into gear and head toward the hospital, still not sure whether getting involved in the life of the Miller men is a smart move or not.

Once bitten, twice shy.

At least one good thing came from this morning.

Now I know where I can take Ryan.

CHAPTER 7 – "LONELIEST SOUL"

Sean

Sitting in my home office, I should be working on my complex takeover case. Instead, I'm staring out the window overlooking Lake Shore East Park spread out before me. It's Thursday lunch time and the park is bustling with office workers escaping the confines of their tall towers for fresh air and sunshine. The thought that people feel like getting outside into the fresh air gives them a sense of freedom makes me smile. I used to be like that, an intern, then an associate, and years before my time, a partner. Now I can charge high, hit low, and generally determine whether a case sees the inside of a courtroom or not. It's been hard going, but all of my work has paid off, despite the loss of my parents, the loss of my grandparents, the loss of …

Anyway, now the only thing—the only person I have to deal with—is Ryan.

I look at the clock hanging on my office wall, Ryan must be released by now. I don't know this because Ryan called me and asked me to pick him up, but from the billing clerk who called a few hours ago wanting details for payment. Of course, I paid it, I always pay where Ryan is concerned. Whether with money or with pride, someone always pays.

I lean back in my leather chair, lifting my legs up and resting them on the top of my desk, my ankles crossed as I grab my cup of coffee and reflect on where my life is going. I'm thirty-four years old in a month. Thirty-four with a million dollar view, a successful career and a nightclub that keeps rising in popularity but what else do I have?

What would my grandfather think of my life? He was a fair man, a good man who believed in reaping the rewards of hard work and who tried to instil the same philosophy in both of us, but Ryan was never the type of person who wanted to work hard to get what he wanted. Even as a young boy he sought instant gratification.

Maybe that is why gambling has become his addiction of choice. I know, he could have chosen much worse, but when his addiction and his need to be saved encroaches on my time and my business, I have to cut my losses. Brother or not, he needs to save himself, stand on his own two feet and not have me and everything my hard work has earned propping him up.

But old habits never die and I'm wondering where Ryan is going to go. I put in a call to his landlord on Tuesday morning and paid for this month's rent and the month he was in arrears. That's not to say I won't make him work his ass off to pay me back for it, but I'm not heartless enough to leave him homeless either. I've contacted his old therapist as well and she's sending me details regarding local Gamblers Anonymous meetings for him to go to. I can't force him to get help, but if he wants any help from me he'll need to take action. Doing something about paying back his debts would be a good start, but once he's recuperated and back home, I'll swing by and have a talk.

My outburst at the hospital still stands true though. I'm sick of being stuck in a parent role instead of a brother role which means that something has to change. I'm just hoping that Ryan will take the initiative this time, with a little encouragement from me.

The doorbell snaps me out of my thoughts. I take a sip from my coffee and switch screens on my monitor, almost spitting out the contents when I see Samantha and Ryan standing at the front door to my condo. I stare at the screen in shock but not because of Ryan. It's the fact that he's with Sammy, my Sammy, that is the kicker.

I thought it was strange that she'd turned up at the hospital the other night to check on him, but pleased as hell that she had and I got the chance to see her again. I meant every word when I said I'd see her soon, but two days later with my brother on my doorstep wasn't on the cards.

Making my way down into the living area, then down the wooden stairs to the entranceway, I hesitate for a moment, sucking back the anger I still feel for Ryan while trying to work out what the hell he's playing at by bringing Sam to my doorstep. Not for my sake, of course, but for hers.

I open the door and her radiant eyes captivate me once again. "Samantha, nice to see you again. Twice in a week is a pleasant surprise." I look past her to see a sheepish Ryan holding a bag to his chest. His eyes are glued to the ground, refusing to meet mine. "Ryan," I say in a low, strained voice.

Samantha clears her throat and looks me square in the eye. "Look. I know you weren't expecting us, but when I called your office they said—"

My head jerks back. "You rang my office?"

"Yeah, they said you were working from home, so when Ryan told me that he couldn't go back to his place right now, I thought it would be okay to come here."

I shoot Ryan a menacing look before ushering them both inside. Ryan goes first, followed by Sam. I don't miss the opportunity that presents itself to check out her perfect, peach shaped ass. Images of rubbing my hands over the soft orbs flash in my mind and I have to think of cold showers and wrinkly old ladies to calm the blood that's rushing south of my belt. Amazing that she still affects me like that.

When we reach the living area, I walk behind the kitchen counter, buying myself some time to will my body back into a more relaxed state. Ryan stops by the counter and drops his bag on the floor before taking a stool. To be honest, he looks worn out. He couldn't have gotten out of hospital more than an hour ago.

"Would you two like a drink? Coffee, juice, wine maybe?"

Ryan looks up at me suspiciously, his brow raised in silent question.

"Beer, Ry?" I watch him lift his chin before I cut across to Sam who politely shakes her head and takes a seat on my black leather sofa. I grab a beer out of the fridge and pop the cap with an opener from the drawer before handing it to Ryan. I brace myself on the counter and take a deep breath, mentally preparing myself for whatever I'm about to be told.

"How are you feeling?" I ask when he finally meets my eyes.

"Better. Still sore, but the doc says I should be fine for work next week." I nod in agreement before turning to Sam.

"Ryan, do you want to go first?" Sam asks. He shakes his head and takes a long swig of beer. I study him, recognizing all the signs of a man who has yet to accept the consequences of his actions. Seems my ultimatum at the hospital had no effect. My mood starts to darken when I hear Sam's soft voice filter through the silence again.

"All right. Well, Ryan called me this morning because he couldn't call you. His stuff was at the bar, and he asked me to pick him up. I made the decision to call your office and when I was told you were working from home, I asked Ryan for your address and here we are." She's got her cop hat on. As much as her professionalism is honorable, it pisses me off when it's directed at me of all people.

"How can I help then?" I bite out, gritting my teeth. The room is full of tension. I can see Ryan in my peripheral vision, his hand gripping his bottle like his life depends on it.

"Well …" She fidgets in the seat. "In the car, Ryan explained how he doesn't feel safe at his apartment due to whatever is going on with him. He has explained that he has an addiction problem and that he'd like to get some help." The more she talks, the stronger her demeanor becomes. She's found her stride now and I couldn't be prouder. "I think Ryan should stay with you." I open my mouth to argue, but she doesn't stop talking. "And when he's feeling physically stronger, you can both sit down and discuss what his options are regarding therapy, Gamblers Anonymous or similar, and whether he still has a job."

I stare at her. Everything I was going to talk to Ryan about so that he can get help for his addiction, has already been covered by Sam in the short trip from the hospital. The woman in front of me has miraculously achieved what I couldn't in the past, which is to get Ryan to agree.

Turning toward Ryan, I notice he has visibly relaxed since Sam finished her spiel. I can't help softening my stance when I realize that he was genuinely worried that I wouldn't help him. Maybe he did take my words seriously the other night.

"Okay."

"Okay?" he pipes up, his voice croaky and full of unspoken emotion.

"Yes, Ry. You can stay here for a few days. Your rent is up to date and paid for the next month, and your landlord has recently upgraded the security system, so I'm sure you will be safe there, but you have just been released from the hospital with a few cracked ribs and a head wound. You can stay in the guest room beside my office until you're back on your feet, but there will be no visitors, no computer, no cell. No access to betting of any sort. This is me giving my little brother one last chance since today you've given me a ray of hope that you can see this through this time."

He nods. "Thanks, brother. I'm beat. I'm going to go lie down if that's okay."

"Good idea. I'll wake you before I leave for the club. Maybe we'll have dinner?"

"Great." His voice is decidedly more upbeat when he answers. He stands and picks up his bag, turning toward Sam. "Thanks, Sammy, I really appreciate you picking me up."

"You're welcome, Ryan. I'll call in a few days to check on you." The smile she gives him blinds me. I'm hit with memories of all the times she'd looked at me like that. It's like a sucker punch to my very being. I want that smile directed at me again, and fuck if I'm not going to use every weapon in my arsenal to make that happen.

Once Ryan has left, she stands up and I have to choose whether to let her go again or press my case.

I walk around the counter and casually lean against it, never taking my eyes off her. She noticeably shudders under my gaze and drops her eyes before her body stills, realizing what she just did. She turns away from me and walks over to my floor-to-ceiling windows overlooking the street and park.

"Surely this isn't another coincidence, Samantha. The hospital was chance, but this time you knew you'd be seeing me again …"

"I'm helping Ryan," she replies a bit too quickly.

As always, she's wearing her heart on her sleeve. She was never able to hide her emotions very well, something I know has been used to her disadvantage in the past. The demise of our relationship case in point. "And I appreciate that, but Ryan is a big boy who needs to stand on his own two feet. Something I told him the other night before I saw you in the corridor."

"Sean, he needs help. He's your brother, your only family."

"I'm perfectly aware of that fact but it goes both ways. What I'm wondering is when do I say enough is enough?"

"When there are no other options."

"Is that what you did, Sammy?"

"What?" she splutters defensively, turning around to face me.

I stand up straight, pulling my shoulders back, preparing for one of two scenarios to play out.

1) She bolts.

or

2) She stands up to me.

Neither one will deter me or turn me off if I'm honest.

"When you ended things between us?"

"That was ten years ago …"

"It was, yet seeing you again after all this time has made me remember what happened between us …" I leave the statement unfinished as I step closer and her eyes go wide, then dart toward the stairwell leading down to the entranceway. I shake my head at her as I recognize her flight reflex threatening to kick in. "Uh-uh, Samantha. There's no escape this time. I let you walk once, and I'm not too keen on seeing the woman who is still buried deep under my skin disappear for another ten years without some answers."

"Sean, I—"

I stop a foot away from her, putting my hands in my pockets as I trail my eyes from her feet up her long, tanned legs, to her sexy as hell cut-off black denim shorts, her jade fitted tee, to an all too familiar emerald pendant hanging from a silver chain around her neck. I quickly try to hide my shock. She still has the necklace I gave her on our one year anniversary. The same one I was given by my grandmother to give to her. A piece of my heart that she kept close to her own despite walking away from me, *from us*, all those years ago. Surely this can't be a coincidence.

My perusal stops when my eyes meet hers and I can't help but smirk when her eyes drop to the floor moments later, but not before I see that spark that I caught a glimpse of the other night, a flash of recognition that I see right through her defenses.

Realizing she's cornered, she changes tactics. "Look, I just wanted to get

Ryan settled and it looks like he is so I better get going. I've got a lot to do before I start work again tomorrow." She looks up at me, donning a fake smile that doesn't reach her eyes before making a step to the side to pass by me.

I shoot my arm out and gently grab her bicep. "Sammy," I murmur in a low, controlled voice. We both look down at my hand touching her bare skin, the electricity sparking between us like an arcing current buzzing between two power sources—the strength of the connection thrilling yet shocking. I watch her chest rise and fall, her breaths coming short and fast.

"You can continue to deny this, but I'm not going away this time. I'm not going to let you walk away without at least having dinner with me."

"What?"

"Dinner. Two people meeting in a public restaurant where they enjoy a meal and maybe a glass or two of wine. They converse, they laugh, they share what's been going on in their lives for the past decade. It's a common pastime I'm led to believe." I don't try to hide the veiled humor in my voice. Her reaction tells me that she's very much attuned to me and my nature, and that she's fully aware of what she is, yet trying to deny that fact. But she's failed to hide her still existing attraction to me. That much is obvious.

"I'm very aware of what dinner is," she snaps.

I grin at the sudden rediscovery of her backbone. "Then you'll meet me this week for a meal? For old times' sake. A toast to old friends."

"We were never just friends, Sean."

"No, we weren't." My reply is direct and forceful, my voice strong and unwavering. "But I'm hoping to find out where we stand now because Sammy …" I release her arm and step in front of her, our bodies so close that I can feel the heat radiating off her, but she just stares at my chest, her brows furrowed as she visibly tries to process our close proximity. "I fully intend to find out what you've learned in the years we've been apart. Whether your eyes still turn dark when I use words to caress your soul. Whether you're as breathtaking as you always were when I turn you on and finally …" I stop and lift my hand between us, using my index finger to lift her chin until she meets my gaze. The desire I'm feeling reflects back at me from her eyes, and I bite back a groan when her tongue darts out, licking her parted lips. Our eyes lock together, neither one of us willing or wanting to pull away. It hits me that the pull this woman has over me is as strong as it ever was.

When I continue, my voice is low and full of grit. "I want to know whether you'll still scream my name until your voice is hoarse when my mouth is on you …" I lean in to place a gentle lingering kiss on her soft red lips before kissing her cheek with the same treatment, then whispering in her ear, "Whether you'll still tremble when my cock's buried deep inside you, our bodies so close you can't tell where yours ends and mine begins."

Her eyes turn dark and her body unconsciously leans toward mine, and I realize that if I don't end this now, I'll push her too far, too fast. I take a step back and try to reel in the unbridled desire pulsing through my body. She looks down and sees exactly how I'm feeling right now, and when her eyes snap back to mine I decide to press my case, using all the confidence and bravado I'm known for in the courtroom.

"But these are all things we can discuss at dinner. I'll call you with the reservation details. Now I must check on my impromptu house guest before I get back to my case. Do you need me to show you the way out?"

She looks at me a heartbeat too long before breathlessly answering, "No."

Fuck if I don't feel that deep in my groin.

I give a short sharp nod of approval before spinning on my heel and walking toward the hallway. The string may be stretching between us as I leave but not once do I feel it snap and recoil.

My week is suddenly looking brighter.

CHAPTER 8 – "CAN'T REMEMBER TO FORGET YOU"

Sam

"What the fuck was I thinking, Helen? Dinner with Sean? That's it. I'm calling to cancel."

"No, you're fucking not. You're going to finish getting dressed, you're going to go to that restaurant, and you're going to show Sean Miller that you are even more of a knockout than you used to be. You're going to sit down and have a friendly meal with the man. You'll be cordial, witty, charming, and funny. All of the things we both know you can be. You're not going to shut down on him, you're not going to brush him off and, repeat after me, you're not going to go to bed with him."

"But … what?"

"You heard me …"

"Helen, like hell that is going to happen. This is a dinner between old friends."

"You two were never old friends. You were made for each other. Well, I thought so until the lingering doubts in your head were fed and cultivated and you fucked it all up."

"Why am I friends with you again?" I ask, half serious and half deflecting. She's right, of course, but I'm pushing back the need to admit that she's one hundred percent right.

"Because you love me and I'm the annoying voice of reason at the back of your head that you need to hear when you're thinking about being a dumbass." She giggles and I struggle to hold back a smile.

"See! That's what you needed to hear. A good ol' Helen pep talk before the big game."

"Game?"

"You and Sean. I'd love to be a fly on the wall in the restaurant. I just know the sexual tension is going to be epic." She claps her hands in glee. "I'm kind of glad there is finally a man with brass balls in your life again."

"Helen!" I growl.

"What? You cannot tell me that Tanner is not a pussycat in the sack. I've seen that guy around and I've seen him around you. He's a pussy whipped sap who would let you spank his ass and literally bust his balls."

"He is not a pussycat in the sack. He's a pussycat out of bed," I retort with a smirk.

I think back to last night when Tanner had turned up on my doorstep, disrupting me from my CSI New York episode. "Tanner," I mumbled through a yawn as I answered the front door wearing a tank top, pajama shorts and purple fluffy slippers. Turning up unannounced was not an uncommon occurrence for him, but knowing that I had dinner with Sean the next night, I wasn't in the mood for company. My mind changed when he presented me with a tub of Ben & Jerry's 'Karamel Sutra' ice cream. He had the cutest grin on his face, so I couldn't turn him away after that, could I?

"Baby, you didn't reply to my text so I thought I'd head over with dessert. That's okay, right?"

Tanner, the sweet, hot as fuck, sensitive new aged guy who's been a frequent inhabitant in my bed for the past few months. He caught my eye when I was at the academy working as a field training officer. I'd needed a work out and decided to join in with a bunch of recruits who were working their way through circuit training. When Tanner knelt in front of me and held my feet down while I did sit ups, it was one of those swoon worthy moments where our eyes met, the air crackled between us, and his huge white smile did me in.

Much to Tanner's chagrin, I could only offer him a physical relationship, not an emotional one. We went out for a drink after work where I explained this to him. After the impromptu date, he was the perfect gentleman and walked me to my door. He then moved toward me, forcing me back until my body was flush against the wood paneling of the doorway and proceeded to kiss the shit out of me. It was soft, almost cautious at first, then the moment I opened my mouth to him, he went in for the kill. Long, languid strokes of his tongue explored my mouth with such enthusiasm and passion I was left a panting mess when he finally pulled away, resting his head against my forehead while he recovered. When I whispered in his ear, asking if he wanted to come inside, he stood up straight and looked down at me. His eyes widened in surprise before he reached around me and pushed the door open. He gently moved me inside and shut the door behind us. I don't think we made it to the bedroom that first time, or the second. By the third round, we were at the slow, lazy, sleepy sex stage and the bed was the most comfortable place to be.

That was the first night of many that Tanner and I ended up in bed together. We occasionally work out together, we share a meal once in a while, and we've attended work functions as the other's plus one, but it's always been a 'friends with benefits' situation. I didn't go after an arrangement like the one we have, but it fits into my life perfectly. I know Tanner wants more, he's always wanted more, and I don't miss the looks of adoration he shoots my way when he thinks I'm not looking.

But Tanner, for all his fantastic qualities in and out of the bedroom, is not who my heart truly desires. He makes me hot, but he doesn't make my blood boil. He has the stamina of a teenager and can provide encore performances over and over again, but he doesn't have me panting with need, desperate to be touched and begging to be taken.

Only one man has ever had that effect on me. And my reaction to him as well as ideas that were planted in my head that I allowed to take root, is why I ran from him all those years ago. Not that he knows that.

Having already had a memorable visit with Sean earlier in the day, when Tanner moved close to me on the couch and started stroking my bare leg, moving his fingers in tender, wide circles higher and higher, I had to put a stop to it. There was no way I could sleep with Tanner when the only man in my head was a dark haired, blue-eyed dominant who had my body burning with spoken words and unspoken promises.

So here I am, 7.30 p.m. on a Friday night, putting the final touches of my makeup on while Helen acts as the good angel on my shoulder. Sean called me yesterday afternoon saying that he had an eight o'clock reservation for us. When I tried to probe him for more information, he chuckled and called my enthusiasm endearing.

For the record, Sean chuckling … actually, anything resembling laughter from him is as rare as a Sasquatch sighting. It happens, but the occurrences are so few and far between that it's a beautiful sight to see and hear when he did. It's not that he was so tightly strung that he couldn't laugh, or didn't want to. No, the Sean of my past had an intensity about him, a presence that you felt whenever he was in the room with you. He was like a silent assassin. He would sit back and study people, trying to get a read of them without uttering a single word. And from what I've seen of the Sean of today, that intensity has increased tenfold with a carnal edge that is just too much to take … yet so irresistible.

"Earth to Sammmmmm," Helen calls out teasingly as I'm snapped back into reality.

I shake my head to clear Sean from my head momentarily.

"Sam, seriously hon. Don't overthink this. Just go with your gut. As you said, even though I don't believe you, this is just two friends having dinner and catching up on what they've missed. Just be careful, okay? And whatever you do, don't let what you did in the past stop you from doing anything now. Regret is a pointless emotion unless you learn something from it. In your case, you—"

"I learned not to listen to everything I'm told and to make up my own goddamned mind instead of listening to others," I finish for her.

She stands up from my bed where she has been lying down and walks over to the dresser where I'm getting ready. Standing behind me, she puts her hand on my forearm and looks at me in the mirror. Her gaze softens, her eyes full of understanding. "You know ..."

"Yep," I reply. "Figured that one out after the damage had been done. But by then, I'd already seen him at the dorm party with Jennifer Murray and the rest, they say, is history. You'd remember that night. You were the one I came crying to." I smile half-heartedly at her and she gives me a gentle squeeze of encouragement just as my front doorbell rings.

"Well, there's no Jennifer hanging around now, is there?" She wiggles her eyebrows and we both crack up laughing.

CHAPTER 9 – "SORRY SEEMS TO BE THE HARDEST WORD"

Sean

All day I've been willing time to speed up. When I last saw Sammy she was standing in the middle of my living room looking stunned, speechless, and turned on. When I rang her yesterday to confirm dinner for tonight, she sounded surprised that I'd called so soon. Strangely enough, she never asked how I got her number. I guess she assumed I got it off Ryan.

Speaking of my errant baby brother, he's stuck to himself the past two days. We've arranged for him to return to work next Tuesday, and this weekend I'll be sitting down with my PI to put some measures in place to protect myself in case things start to turn south. I've already asked him to look into Ryan's affairs and try to find out exactly what and who we're dealing with and I'm hoping he'll have some answers for me when we meet.

Until then, I have the company of the delectable Miss Richards to look forward to. I'm not nervous about dinner. In fact, I'm looking forward to finding out all that has happened in her life since we broke up.

It may seem like this huge mystery as to why Sam ended our relationship and never spoke to me again, but that's because it is a mystery—to me. But I hope to learn a lot more about that by reconnecting with her again. However, I meant every word I said to her yesterday. Seeing her again has reignited something inside of me, something that was snuffed out a long time ago. I need Sam in my life; she brings color to an otherwise black and white world. Now don't get me wrong, I'm not unhappy or depressed, I've got a successful career, a thriving club, and I'm never short on options for female companionship. The thing is, I never realized how much I was settling until I saw Sam again.

She is more radiant, more magnificent than she ever was. When I first met her, Samantha Richards took my breath away. Yesterday, seeing her in my house in painted on jeans and a tight tee, she was an instant fucking hard on wrapped up in fabric.

Now I'm in a town car headed toward her apartment. All of a sudden, my stomach tightens and for the first time in years I feel nervous as I walk up the few steps to her door.

She opens the door just as I reach the top step and I'm frozen on the spot as I take her in. Her sun-colored hair is tied back in a high ponytail, and I swear that her flawless face is more beautiful than yesterday. My heart stutters as my gaze moves down her body which is covered in a simple yet elegant red dress. Her matching red heels make her silky smooth legs look impossibly long, which just leads my heated stare back over the curve of her hips and the swell of her breasts before meeting her eyes again. Then I see the impish gleam in her eye and it becomes glaringly obvious that she's succeeded in her desire in driving me to distraction. All of it reaffirms to me the fact that I want Sam back in my life.

"You look gorgeous." My gravelly voice resonates between us as I try to recover my scattered thoughts. She unravels me and she doesn't even realize.

Looking to the ground, she blushes, obviously uncomfortable with my compliment. It makes me wonder what kind of men she's had in her life since me. I was taught by my grandfather that a man worth anything at all will tell a woman how much he adores her, showing her with his actions that he's the luckiest son of a bitch on earth to be with her.

And right now, I want to be that son of a bitch.

"Your carriage awaits." She looks up and past my shoulder at the car idling at the curb.

"Oh, right … just let me lock up." I smirk, loving that she's off balance again. "What can I say? Once a cop, always a cop."

"It suits you, you know. It makes sense. I always wondered what you pursued after college."

She turns and hurriedly locks the door, spinning back around to face me. I need to touch her again. The fleeting moment between us yesterday was not enough. All night, instead of focusing on my upcoming case, I was thinking of all the things I wanted to do to her. I dreamed of touching her, exploring every inch of her skin, tasting her …

"Hey, are you okay?" she asks, snapping me out of my thoughts and I realize she's taken a step toward me. "You were a million miles away."

"Sorry. You've kind of thrown me for a loop." I lean forward, placing my hands on her bare shoulders and slowly stroking down her skin, leaving a trail of goose bumps in their wake. Our eyes stay locked as I move back to cup her shoulders and I clear my throat, trying to strengthen my resolve to get answers from her. "We should go before I make a whole new set of plans, and none of them involve dinner."

"Yes, let's go," she replies quickly. I take her hand and give her a light reassuring squeeze before I lead her down into the car.

Once the car is on its way, she pulls her hand away and inconspicuously places it back in her lap.

I see her shoulders straighten as she turns toward me. "So where are we going? You were rather mysterious on the phone."

"Well, I remember a long time ago we talked about traveling, and you always said you wanted to travel around Africa." I raise my brow, waiting for her affirmation and she nods, a sly smile graces her lips. "That's why we're heading to a great Ethiopian restaurant one of the partners recommended."

"Oh wow…if it's the one I'm thinking of, I've wanted to go there forever." I grin at the emergence of goofy Sam. Her true nature, the one I suspect she endeavors to hide away from most people, is one of her most endearing qualities. She was always one of the most 'real' people I knew, no pretenses and no falsities; what you see is what you get with Sam.

One of the biggest issues in our relationship was Sam's submissive side, a wrongly perceived weakness that was preyed upon by someone who should have known better than to meddle in other people's lives.

And tonight, I plan on finding out exactly why that happened.

Sam

My body is on fire.

Ever since he picked me up, I've felt off balance. And now he's being thoughtful and even remembered that I want to travel around Africa. I mean, I haven't seen him for ten years since we broke up, and it wasn't exactly a nice break up either. It was a clean break but with no warning, and I had really shit timing too. To be honest, I'm wondering why he even wants anything to do with me. Does time heal all wounds?

His touch on my skin simply stoked the fire that has grown from a deep buried ember. I still know that there are huge fundamental differences between Sean and I. He is a dominant who likes to control and manipulate women, and I'm a woman who doesn't want to be controlled. See, insurmountable differences that I'm unsure a simple dinner can erase. But then there is the other part of me that relishes in his dominance. The way he takes control of a situation, like paying Ryan's rent and making sure that he's safe despite vowing to never bail out his brother again. Or turning up on my doorstep and telling me that I deserve a man who showers me with compliments and acts like a man who deserves to be with me.

Major swoon factor there.

Now we're walking hand in hand (again) into one of the city's top restaurants. So not where I thought I'd be two days ago.

The maître d' shows us to a corner table near the back and Sean pulls out a chair facing away from the door. It goes against all my trained instincts, but I push them aside and sit down, unable to hold back the shiver that wracks my body when his hands graze my side, stopping just below my breasts.

Once Sean takes his seat opposite, the maître d' lights a single red candle sitting in the middle of the table. "Your waiter for the evening will see you shortly. Have a great night."

"Thank you," Sean says, not taking his eyes off me. His presence still consumes me. He may be sitting a few feet away from me, but I can still feel his touch like an invisible brand that warms my skin and seeps through me. It's confusing. My brain, the sane part of it anyway, knows that this is a dinner between two old friends. As much as Helen tells me otherwise, surely that is all it can be. It doesn't matter the effect Sean has on me or my body, or the natural way he can bring out my passive side with a single smoldering stare. It definitely has nothing to do with the fact I'd rather be somewhere less public and more naked with him. No, that has nothing to do with it.

To distract my mind from these befuddling thoughts, I scan my surroundings, falling back on my habit of always being on the job.

Although it's busy, the restaurant's atmosphere is warm and welcoming. The worn wooden floors are polished to perfection, and multi-colored pastel draped curtains line the floor to ceiling windows along the street front. Then there are the table dressings. Crisp white tablecloths perfectly pleated with two crystal clear water glasses filled with a rolled, blood-red napkin. Every care has been taken, and the attention to detail is flawless.

"Samantha, would you like me to order some wine?" Sean's deep voice rumbles through me. I look back over at him, giving him the gentlest of smiles.

"Sure, that would be nice." He nods and picks up the menu, perusing it with a concentrated frown, only looking up when our waiter stops at his side.

"Would you like to order some drinks?" the young man asks us both.

"Yes, I'd like to order a bottle of the Indaba Sauvignon Blanc, please. And if I could order our meal as well, we'll have the Messob sampler." He closes the menu and places it in the waiter's outstretched hand.

"Your wine will be brought to your table shortly, sir." He looks at me briefly, "Madam," then leaves.

I stare at Sean in shock. In barely a minute he's ordered our drinks and meal without even stopping to consider that I might want to order something different. There is being a gentleman and asking if he can order on your behalf, then there is steamrolling your dinner date and taking over. Sean is obviously a believer in the second philosophy.

"Did you consider that I might want to order something for myself?" I ask incredulously, unable to hold back my disbelief.

He looks at me with eyes dancing with amusement. What the fuck is funny with what I just said? "I'm sorry, Samantha. Old habits die hard. You always used to like it when I ordered for the both of us."

I open my mouth to voice an objection but stop mid gape. Surely he can't be serious. "Sean, that was ten years ago. People do change you know." I point a finger at my chest. "For example, me."

He chuckles and leans back in his seat, still amused at my reaction. "I've apologized already, and I'm not going to do it again. If you would like, we'll change the order when the waiter returns. I simply thought you'd enjoy the choices that the sampler provides. It is a three course dinner with sambussa, messob and dessert. The full Ethiopian dining experience. I was just trying to cover all bases."

Well, fuck! How can I argue with that? My previously squared shoulders relax as I give up the fight over a stupid dinner order. I don't know what tonight is about, but I have a feeling from Sean's confident demeanor that he has everything planned out. He always has to know what is going to happen and when. To put it plainly, he is a hard man to surprise.

"I'm sorry. I'm just nervous I guess."

"Nervous, Sammy?"

I don't think I'll ever get used to him calling me Sammy again, his pet name for me. In two days he has made my world shift on its axis with promises of seeing me again, and yesterday's declaration where he told me in no uncertain terms that he wants to taste, touch and hear me as I come. Shit, is it getting hot in here?

"A bit I guess," I reply honestly. "But you were always one to keep me on my toes and I've realized that is something that hasn't changed either." I watch in fascination as his head falls back and roars with laughter, looking more at ease than he has all evening. His laughter dies down to a quiet chuckle as he grins over the table at me. "Shit, I needed that. Thank you."

I shrug my shoulders but can't hide the sly smile on my face as I look out the window of the restaurant, trying to appear unaffected by the nothing short of dazzling man across from me. But if I thought I was succeeding, the intense heated stare Sean gives me in response negates that. Thankfully we're interrupted by the waiter returning with our wine. He uncorks the bottle, pouring a little splash in Sean's glass before holding it out to him to taste. I watch intently as he lifts the glass to his mouth, pausing to smell the aroma of the wine before parting his lips and tasting the wine. He lowers the glass and locks eyes with me across the table, running his tongue along the inside rim which causing me to squeeze my legs together. I curse the gods for subjecting me to this scene. I'm feeling so hot I'm starting to think I am in Africa.

Dammit! I knew I should have taken the edge off before Sean picked me up. Now I'm sexualizing everything the man does. I mean, he's just tasting the wine and I'm picturing his lips tasting wine from another vessel … me. He shoots me a sexy knowing smirk. Damn mind reader!

He nods and holds his glass out to the waiter who proceeds to fill it, then shifts to my glass, pouring the cool, pale-yellow liquid before bowing slightly and leaving us alone once more.

Sean picks up his glass and holds it up. "To old friends and new beginnings." I clink the crystal against his and bring the edge of the glass to my mouth, my senses scattered between the sensory assault of the wine and Sean's words full of unspoken meaning.

"So tell me what you've been up to for the past decade. I was surprised but not shocked when you told me you were a police officer." He rests his arm of the table, the other hand held close to his chest as he cradles his wine glass. He's the poster boy for relaxed and carefree right now and it secretly irks me because inside I'm a contradiction of feelings— annoyance to lust, and regret to wonder at the difference a decade can make. He clears his throat, and again I'm brought back to reality.

"Uh, yeah," I reply with a smile. "After college I needed a change of scenery and had always intended to look at enforcement of some kind. It just happens that the CPD accepted me."

He nods. "And you enjoy your work?"

I take another long sip of wine to quench my parched throat before answering. "Definitely. I wouldn't do it otherwise. It's fulfilling. I like to think I'm making a difference."

His expression turns from interest to one full of respect. "I can definitely see you relishing that role. And look how it has brought us back full circle. The two of us, together … having dinner … just two old friends reminiscing."

"And an errant younger brother who never learns?"

He chuckles. "An unfortunate event that resulted in a positive outcome for at least one of the Miller men. The jury is still out on the fate of the other one."

I smile and decide it's now or never if I want to find out about the Sean of my past. "And how about you? After pre-law you stayed in Chicago?"

"I kind of had to with Ryan and his never ending brushes with trouble. And after our grandfather passed, it just seemed right to stay in the house for a while. We still have it. I rent it to a nice family who take cares of it as if it's their own."

And just like that, the elephant in the room makes its quiet entrance.

Knowing it wasn't intentional, I side step the pang of guilt that sucker punches me at the mention of his grandfather's death. "I was sorry to hear about your grandfather's passing."

He nods but doesn't speak, his eyes are a different story. They narrow and he tilts his head to the side as if he's studying me. Feeling unsettled and under the spotlight I continue talking, chastising myself for being so paranoid and tense. "And corporate law? You were looking at criminal practice initially …"

"Mmm hmm. But things change, people change. Corporate law seemed to fit me better. Just like law enforcement seems to fit you."

I murmur my agreement. I keep picking up on veiled hints of our past, and what I think are subtle barbs disguised as polite conversation. I'm distracted and mentally weighing his words when I'm saved by the bell, or in this case, saved by the waiter bringing us our appetizers.

As we begin to eat, the silence stretches between us. But by GOD is the food delicious. I swear I'm on the verge of a food orgasm. The wonderful mix of flavors are heaven sent.

When we're finished the appetizers and our plates are taken away, I feel exposed and vulnerable. No, it's not that I don't trust the man in front of me. I always did, implicitly. No, I feel emotionally bare, defenseless and open for interrogation. And of course, Sean is not one to disappoint.

"So is there a special man in your life?" he asks, the twitch in his tightened jaw a dead giveaway that the thought grates on him.

Feeling emboldened by the wine, I decide to be completely honest with him, knowing that I'll be goading a reaction out of him. "Do you think I'd be here if I did?" I reply with a sly smirk. He quirks a brow and I swallow hard before continuing. "There's someone who I enjoy uncommitted benefits with, but I have no time or inclination for anything more permanent. My career is what is important to me right now."

His eyes darken and I swear I hear a growl from his side of the table. "What's his name?" he asks, his voice low and menacing.

"Tanner. Why?" A thrill goes through me at his reaction to another man in my life, and it confuses the hell out of me.

Our main selection arrives and I know this may be my last chance to find out the one thing that has been eating away at me since I first saw Sean again at the hospital. "And how about you, Sean? Any special lady?"

He doesn't even flinch at the question, answering without hesitation. "No. My heart was well and truly done for by one woman a long time ago. Haven't had the time or desire to try for anything else since."

I fill my fork with food and stuff my mouth with it, willing the earth to swallow me up whole. This conversation is fucking with my head and my emotions.

Thankfully, we're soon too busy eating to continue the interrogation. It's not to say that we don't exchange pleasantries and light banter. That side of things was always easy for the two of us. Our issues stem from the deeper stuff, the wants and desires and hopes for the future. Or more importantly, my denial about my sexual submissiveness. There's also the fact that I let someone who should have known better poison my mind and belittle the love I had for him, twisting it into something I was told I had no business selling myself short for.

By the time our plates are cleared away at the end of the meal, and the bottle of wine has been long emptied, I'm too blissed out from the food orgy I've just experienced to notice a shift in Sean's mood. He calls for the bill, and hands over his platinum card to the Maître d' before standing up, holding out his hand and pulling me up until my body is flush with his.

"I had a good time tonight. But I'm still wondering why we had to miss out on ten years of spending time together like this. If you're agreeable, I'd like to walk off some of this food stupor and talk honestly with each other about what happened back then." He places his hand on the small of my back and pushes firmly. Without realizing, I'm soon moving forward and walking out the front door with him.

As soon as the cool night air hits my skin I freeze, realizing what just happened. This is what I'd been wanting to avoid. This is what I didn't want to face. He watches me intently, not missing the moment my body goes rigid.

"I … uh …"

"Sammy." There goes that name again. The one that has the power to turn me to mush in two syllables. I feel the tension in my body ease slightly and automatically lean toward him. His eyes soften as he continues, "I'm not going to tie you up and spank you, Sam … well, not until you admit you want me to. Even if the thought of your red glowing ass under my hand turns me on …"

That instantly gets my back up again. Who the hell does he think he is saying he wants to spank my ass red? That's going too damn far.

I cannot deny that there have been times over the years when I have contemplated looking Sean up, but I've always stopped myself before googling his name because of the shame I feel when I think back to what I did. And now he's standing here in all his dominant, commanding, handsome glory asking me to walk with him and talk about what happened.

I just can't do it.

I feel the warmth of his body against mine and the slut part of my brain tries to reason with the rational side that there would be no harm, no foul if I just let Sean have his wicked way with me. Then a small sliver of clear thinking shines through and I realize that I need to get out of this situation and fast. I change from my sexy panties to my bitch panties, pulling back my shoulders and looking him straight in the eye.

"Look, Sean, I appreciate dinner and it has been great to catch up, but I'm not willing to take a walk down memory lane with you and rehash the past. It was good, then it was bad, and now it is great to reconnect, but I think it's best if we just put this down to exactly what you said, two old friends catching up for old times' sake. Now we can move on knowing there is no animosity between us so if we see each other around, it won't be awkward."

Well, that came out better than I could have hoped.

He takes a step back from me and I immediately lose the warm, mellow feeling I had as it transforms into something more closely resembling the hard look that now mars his beautiful face. "Right. So I invite you to a nice, well thought out meal, if I do say so myself. We share a bottle of wine, you clamp up the minute the topic of conversation hits too close to home, and now when I suggest a walk after our wonderful, albeit quiet dinner, you balk and decide it's too hard."

"Well, I—"

"No. You're right. At least one of us can think clearly around the other because I thought that this night would take another turn, maybe lead down a different, definitely more enjoyable path. I was obviously mistaken. I see that your complete inability to be honest with yourself hasn't changed."

Now that got my back up. "Hang on a minute. You can't honestly think that you could bring me out for a nice meal and I'd lie down on my back, spread my legs and put out like some spineless submissive whore. That's barbaric!" I shout, not giving a fuck that we're in the middle of the sidewalk.

His face suddenly cracks into a full arrogant smile before he answers. "Now there's the fire I've been looking for. Fortunately, all I see now is an image of you spread eagled, lying before me, begging me to take you." He leans in until we're almost nose to nose. "Tell me what it'll take to make that happen." He stands up straight and shoots me an arrogant smirk.

Before I know it, my palm connects with his cheek, making my hand sting. "You did not just say that! Seriously, Sean, you are the most arrogant ass of a man I've ever met. You're lucky your hand still wants to touch your own junk. Thank you for the meal, but goodbye and have a nice life!" I turn my back and stride away from him, thankful yet disappointed that he doesn't come after me.

I walk half a block and turn the corner before hailing the first cab I see. Jumping in, I give the driver my address before resting my head on the cool glass window as he pulls back into traffic. Biting my lip, I try to hold back the deluge of emotion threatening to burst out of me.

Damn that man.

CHAPTER 10 – "WALKING AWAY"

Sean

I watch Sam walk away from me as I war with the need to chase after her versus the need to give her the space she so obviously desires. I pushed too hard. I text my car service and five minutes later, a black sedan pulls up to the curb outside the restaurant. Telling him to take me to the club, I drop my head against the back seat and scrub my face with my hands. I fucked up. I'm man enough to admit it, but fuck if I know how to fix it.

I thought dinner had gone well. She was quiet while we ate, answering my questions but focusing on the food more than anything else. There were a few times when I mentioned certain things subconsciously, not realizing how they may have been taken, that I noticed her pause whatever she was doing. A fork laden with food stopping mid-air, or her body tensing up when I mentioned my grandfather's passing. I didn't mean to bring up our past, or the moment when she walked out of my life, but even I know that if Samantha and I are to have any chance of moving forward, we'll need to deal with why she broke up with me and the issues that caused it.

In the ten minute drive to the club, I think back to that day when I met Samantha's mother, the last woman to storm out of a restaurant and leave me speechless …

Which is a big achievement.

We'd met her at the restaurant of her hotel and straight away I knew I was in trouble. Sam had told me on the way there that her mom was stuck in her military ways and that she sometimes had trouble distinguishing between the military way of life and the way Sam chose to live hers. It had always been a bone of contention between them with Sam usually conceding to her mom to keep the peace.

Sam and I had talked about our families when we'd first started dating a year earlier, and Sam had met my brother and my grandparents. I hadn't been introduced to her mother until then because her mom lived in Kentucky. She'd recently retired from the Army and had been based at Fort Knox but was thinking about joining Sam in Chicago, hence the visit.

When we walked to the restaurant I knew we were in trouble. Debra Richards, in her well-polished, rigid stance, was already seated at our table, looking at her watch intently before scanning the room and seeing us. Her furrowed brow at Sam was all the confirmation I needed. Her mom was pissed, and I'd made the worst first impression possible. I should have seen the writing on the wall then and there because the lunch only went from bad to worse after that.

First thing I did wrong was ordering Sam's meal. It was a habit I had gotten into early into our relationship. I knew what she liked and didn't like, and she would just let me order for her whenever we went out. I didn't think twice about it, it was just second nature, but the scowl I got from Debra following a loud unapologetic gasp let me know that I'd fucked up.

"Samantha, I was certain you knew how to order your own meal. Did I not teach you that?"

"Mom, Sean and I know each other well, and he knows what I like, so he orders for me. I find it endearing."

"I find it controlling. Anyway, Sean, Samantha tells me you're studying pre-law with her. Which law schools are you looking at?"

My eyes widened at Debra's directness. She'd been abrupt with me since we'd arrived, yet she'd dived straight in there with the hard questions, questions that Sam and I hadn't discussed in depth between the two of us let alone with her mother that I just met.

"I'm staying at the University of Chicago, Mrs. Richards."

"It's Ms. Richards. I never married the asshat thankfully."

My head shot back in shock at her retort. I held back a grin that I knew would not be appreciated in that moment, but I now knew where Sam got her dirty mouth from. "Sorry," I replied sincerely.

"So you should be." Her eyes narrowed and suddenly I felt like I was on the witness stand at a trial.

"Mom!" Sam admonished, her cheeks glowing red as she hung her head embarrassed. Her hand holding mine in my lap squeezed apologetically and I knew that she was struggling.

"It's okay, Sammy." That earned a raised eyebrow which I ignored as I continued. "Ms. Richards, I applied to the University of Chicago so that I could stay near Samantha."

"Hmm. And Samantha? Have you decided what you're going to do yet?"

She sighs resignedly, looking sideways at me then turning to face her stony-faced mother. "I still have a year to decide, Mom."

"Humph."

Thankfully, our meals arrived after that and Sam was able to steer the conversation toward more popular topics of conversation, namely about her mother's retirement and plans for the future.

The next thing I did wrong was standing up as I was taught to do when Debra excused herself to use the restroom. She frowned at me then left.

"I can't seem to do anything right. I'm thinking it's not just me though," I whispered when her mom was out of hearing range.

"It's not you. It's just the way she is. I'll smooth it all over later. You're doing great. I love you," she added, leaning toward me and kissing me gently, opening her mouth and allowing me to take over. It was a well-practiced dance that we had perfected over time. It was effortless, but still got my blood pumping in mere seconds.

Not realizing Debra had returned, we were interrupted by a stern throat clearing in front of us.

"Oh, shit," Sam muttered. "Sorry, Mom. Didn't realize you had come back."

"Obviously. The young man here couldn't have mauled you in private? Samantha, you know better than to conduct yourself that way in public. I'm no longer hungry. The bill is taken care of, so you needn't worry, Sean." She leaned down and kissed Sam on the cheek before nodding dismissively in my direction. "I'll call you at twenty hundred hours, Samantha."

"Well, that was an epic fuck up," I declared once she had walked away. "Sorry, Sammy, but your mom is an A grade bitch. She disregarded me the minute she clocked me."

She looked at me with those big, wide, green eyes of hers and I could see she was torn. "She's just stressed. She's retired from the job she says she was born to do, and now she's at a loss as to what to do with her life. I'll talk to her tonight. Let's just go."

And just like that, my meet the mother lunch was over and done with.

The car pulls up outside the club which looks busy with a line around the corner at least. Suddenly, the events of the night feel heavy on my shoulders. "Actually, can you take me to my condo? I don't think I should be here right now," I say to the driver.

He pulls out into the traffic and takes me home.

Now all I have to figure out is what the fuck happened with Samantha tonight, and more importantly, what the fuck can I do to fix it.

The one thing I know for sure is that Samantha Richards belongs in my life.

Sam

Me: Hels, I'm screwed!

Helen: Literally?

Me: No! I slapped Sean across the face after a thoroughly enjoyable dinner.

Helen: What the fuck, babe …

Me: It seems like such a blur now, but he was in control all night, then he mentioned going for a walk and I was freaking out because he wanted to talk.

Me: So I said it was great to catch up and now we won't be awkward around each other. He accused me of trying to get out of talking about our past, I denied it. Then he said I still couldn't be honest with myself.

Me: I told him he was barbaric thinking I'd spread my legs for a nice meal. He couldn't get that image out of his head and asked how he could make it happen. So I slapped the arrogant smirk right off his face.

Helen: You finished?

Me: Nope, just getting started. At home now, drinking water because it looks like Vodka and I have a shift tomorrow.

Helen: Lucky you didn't end up spreading your legs then ;)

Me: *snort* Don't see that happening anytime soon.

Helen: I call bullshit, AGAIN. You need to sort your head out and claim your man. Sean IS the kind of man you NEED in your life, babe.

Rico: Sam, you be with who you want to be with. Don't let my fiancée bully you

Me (sent to both of them): What the fuck, guys? Ganging up on me much?

Helen: He stole my phone, blame him. All right, babe, might see you tomorrow. Sleep on it. Think about what that man does to you just by breathing, then you'll have your answer.

Rico: If he breaks your heart, I'll kill him.

Helen: At least tell me the food was good. Rico owes me a date night.

Me: LOL. Food was awesome. Ethiopian restaurant, I'll give you the details tomorrow. Love you guys. Thanks for letting me vent.

Helen: That's what we're here for, babe. Just sleep on it. Everything will be clearer in the morning.

Me: I fucking well hope so. That man pissed me off, turned me on, and scattered my brain all in the space of a few hours.

Helen: So nothing's changed then ;)

Me: Shut up!

Helen: Love you, babe. You're just too pig headed to admit you were wrong and you want him back.

Me: Shut UP!

Helen: ha ha.

Me: Enough. Sleeping now. Have a good shift tomorrow.

Helen: Will do. Night.

Rico: Night.

Me: You guys are ridiculous.

Helen: That's why you love us. Now go to sleep!

I put my phone onto my bedside table, rolling onto my side and burrowing into the comforter. My brain is still wired though, so sleep will not come easily. I know I probably overreacted tonight. Shit. Okay, I did overreact, but that man knows how to push all my buttons. He said he wanted to see the fire inside of me … well, he got that back and then some!

I'm scared of losing that fire by submitting to any man, but especially to Sean. I was raised to always stay strong and independent and to never rely on a man for anything because they're all rat bastards who will let you down. How can I let my guard down when the right man comes along … comes back? What if I can't do it? What if it's been up for so long that I can't remember what it is like to be vulnerable again?

Oh, wait. I do know what that feels like. I feel it every single time I see Sean Miller.

I close my eyes and will my mind to stop spinning, then fall asleep with an image of Sean's deep blue eyes staring at me.

I'm screwed.

CHAPTER 11 – "EVERYTHING WILL CHANGE"

Sam

Four days since I walked away from Sean, which (funnily enough) would make us just about even in 'walking away' stakes. Not that I'm keeping track or anything …

I brushed Tanner off over the weekend. Both Saturday and Sunday he wanted to do something. In fact, he shocked the shit out of me when he asked me out to a movie. A chick flick at that! I let him down easy, saying I was wiped out from work and needed an early night. My guilt stabbed at me all night, but I'm not in the wrong here. Tanner has always known what our deal was. Right from the beginning I'd established boundaries and he was happy with that, or he appeared happy with that.

I mean what man wouldn't be happy with having a woman who's wants just regular, okay very regular non-committal sex and does not, in any way shape or form, want a relationship? My job is my partner. Okay, it doesn't keep me warm at night, nor does it give me love, but Tanner takes care of the nights. As for love, I had it once and it ripped my heart out. I was the instigator of the break up, but when I'd realized my mistake, Sean had moved on. Looking back, I've recognized how big of an idiot I was to listen to my mother's opinion on Sean and my relationship with him. I took something that was built on love and trust and decimated it within mere moments with words that were not my own.

Back then, my doubts about being a submissive or even just submissive to Sean, had always lingered. Sticking at the back of my mind as our relationship progressed from that amazing first date to where we were at the time I broke up with him a year later.

As he explained to me early on, he liked having control during sex. He was not a hard core Dominant, but it was an important aspect of him that I would need to accept if we were to move forward in our relationship. In the beginning, in that glorious honeymoon period where you can't get enough of each other, where you can't stop touching, kissing and making love to each other, Sean eased me into his 'way' of doing things. It was such a heady feeling to give myself to him. It made me feel fulfilled, complete even. In a life where I'd only ever had my mom and the soldiers on the Army base where we lived as role models, I was somewhat exhilarating to have a man want to take care of me the way that Sean did. He cherished me, protected me, looked out for me.

The sex was AMAZING. I'd been with two men before him and there was no comparison. It was like he was the sun and they had been Uranus. I kid you not, the sex was out of this world. But with a mother that raised me the way she did, I always wondered if I was giving a part of myself up when I was with him, a part that was given willingly and without thought.

As natural as breathing.

The day I broke up with him was the most devastating day of my life, but at the time I felt it was necessary.

It was after Sean met my mom for the first time. To say it didn't go well is an understatement. Mom had all but dismissed him from the get go. We arrived late which is something that my mother never appreciated from anyone, but when it was from her daughter's boyfriend it was unforgivable. Then Sean ordered my meal for me and spent the meal with his arm hooked around the back of my chair, things that were natural for us and I actually loved but Mom saw those things differently.

Later that night, when I was in my dorm and called her as requested, she made her unimpressed opinion of Sean very clear.

"Samantha, that boy may be nice, but you are losing yourself to him and that is unacceptable."

"Mom, that is a bit unfair. You spent no more than an hour with him."

"I don't need any more than five minutes to see that the boy is dominating your relationship. No future pairing should be built on an uneven foundation, and what you have with Sean is as crooked as a dog's hind leg. Your father abandoned us the minute you were born, Samantha, and because I was weak, I nearly crumbled. You must stay strong and clear-minded. That man is older than you, headed into a very stressful, powerful career and you're already downtrodden. Get out and end it now."

"He's not like that, Mom. He's—"

"He's domineering, controlling, and disrespectful. You do not need a man like that."

"No! I will not end my relationship with Sean just because you have the wrong idea about him."

"I don't think you're hearing me, young lady. I said you need to end it with him. He is not the right kind of man for you. You need someone who will honor you, support you, and turn up early to the lunch where he's about to meet your mother for the first time. Richards women are no subservient or submissive. We're equal with our men. I wasn't with your father, but I've learned from that mistake. I just don't want you to make the same misguided choices that I made."

"I—"

"No, Samantha. It's simple. Clean break. Do it now before things get more serious."

"I'll think about it."

"No thinking required. Clean break, no harm done. Now, I must go. Early flight in the morning."

"Okay, Mom. It was nice seeing you."

"Call me when you've sorted it out, Samantha. I want better for you."

Later that night when Sean rang me, I'd already been in bed for an hour and was emotionally spent. I blew him off by feigning a headache and promising to catch up with him the next day.

My mother and her toxic opinion of men had successfully fed my doubts about Sean and my relationship. I knew that when I talked to him about it, he would try reasoning with me, but I didn't need handling or psychoanalyzing. All my life I'd been handled in one way or another. What I needed was time and space to think things through.

But I didn't get time and space, and that may just be why things ended the way they did.

On Saturday morning, I receive a call over the radio saying that I have lunch waiting for me at the precinct. Confused but intrigued, Zander and I make our way back to base and walk in to see a bunch of the most beautiful yellow sunflowers I have ever seen on the front desk. Beside the bouquet is a takeaway coffee, a chicken Caesar salad, and a spiced apple muffin.

I think I died and went to heaven in my first bite of that muffin. Of course, there was no note but the desk sergeant told me that a nicely dressed, very handsome man had delivered it and asked that I be told it was there. I didn't need confirmation to know who it was from.

During finals in college, when I was working myself to the bone studying, Sean would stop by with a coffee and a muffin. Of course, I returned the favor by giving him head under his desk, which would lead to him pulling me up from my knees and bending me over said desk …

You get the point.

The smirk on Zander's face is infuriating. "An admirer, Sam?"

"Like you can talk, Roberts. You go pansy faced whenever your girl sends you a text."

His eyes widen slightly before he shakes his head at me, but not before I miss the slight blush of his cheeks. "Anyway, we eating or what?" he asked before heading toward the break room. I chuckle as I follow behind him.

I place the flowers in a cup of water so that they'll last my shift, then put the food on the table and grab my cell from my pocket with the intention of sending a short, sweet text to say thank you.

Me: Hey, it's Sam. I'm guessing the early morning lunch and flower delivery was from you?

Sean: Good guess, Samantha. I want to see you again. We need to clear up last night's miscommunication.

Me: No need. Thank you for the lunch and flowers, they're beautiful. Totally unnecessary.

Sean: Nothing is unnecessary when it comes to you. Let me know when I can see you again.

Holy fuck! I can't respond to that. If there is such a thing as being stunned text-less, that is me.

Sean texts me every night, asking how my day was and reminiscing about specific events in our past. It's disconcerting and thrilling at the same time, like traveling on a roller coaster through time and knowing that the only direction this can go is down, but I can't help myself. It has been nice to reconnect with him. He has asked me to meet with him again, but I've been a coward, continuing to offer up excuses as to why I can't see him.

Texting seems less threatening than a phone call. Don't get me wrong, I still overanalyze his words and the meaning behind them, and agonize over my replies, but it is getting easier. I'm trying to quell the feelings for him that I sense are resurfacing. Honestly, I don't know that I can be the woman he wants, not full time anyway. I admitted to myself a long time ago that although I'm sexually submissive, I'm not into the hardcore kinky shit. I like being restrained, controlled, used by the man I'm with, but it needs to be in the right moment and with the right man. Tanner is not that man, and neither were the few one night stands I've had since Sean.

Remember I said he'd ruined me for other men?

Despite his Saturday delivery last week, and our text conversations since, I'm still the same coward who can't admit she was and is still wrong. It's always been my biggest fault, and with Sean I have more than just the date and my behavior during it to apologize for. How do you say, "Oh, by the way, I'm sorry I fucked up first time around and ruined something fucking awesome between us. Forgive me?"

If only it were that easy.

CHAPTER 12 – "ME & MY JEALOUSY"

Sean

I've found myself at the Chicago Police Memorial Foundation's annual fundraising dinner, representing my firm as a last minute favor for my boss. I haven't brought a date. With more notice, I would have considered asking Samantha, but I know I need to tread lightly with her. Last week's date showed me that I need to be smart in the way I approach her if I want her back in my life … and my bed.

I've had a lot of time to reflect this week on what is missing from my life. Apart from Mac, I haven't wanted a woman for more than a night or two since Sammy, and seeing her again has made me realize that she is the reason why. But in order for me to be sure that she wants to be with me too, she will need to be the one to come to me. I can't force her; I can't make her want to be with me again, but for my peace of mind and for the sake of saving both of us a repeat of the past, she needs to be sure.

That's not to say I can't help her make her mind up though.

My life seems to be un-complicating itself. Well, mainly the part of my life that involves Ryan. He moved back to his apartment earlier this week and has promised to contact both the therapist and Gamblers Anonymous. This time I'm hoping he's been scared enough to get help. There is still the matter of his debt to the bookie who roughed him up in the club—that is one debt I refuse to settle, but if any trouble is made for myself or my club, I promise there will be hell to pay.

I'm sitting at a table with a bunch of old law school buddies of mine when I see her. There may be a lot of beautiful women here, but none of them compare to the sunshine-haired beauty as she walks into the room on the arm of a man who looks like he wants to eat her. I struggle to stifle the growl that rumbles in my chest. My lips tighten, my fists instinctively gripping the table in front of me. She'd told me about Tanner, her casual, not serious fuck buddy, and all indications are that her escort is one and the same. My first instinct is to rip his hands off her; the very thought of any man that isn't me touching her vexes me. I watch with a cold glare as they approach a table with two vacant chairs, smiling at another tall, blond man and his attractive partner who I note has the most striking red hair I have ever seen. He stands and gives Samantha a hug before shaking hands with Tanner and inviting them to sit down. Once Samantha takes her seat— which I'll add, Tanner did NOT pull out for her as a gentleman should—he sits down and drapes his arm possessively along the back of her chair. I subconsciously grind my teeth in frustration. If there was ever a moment to see green, this was it.

In short, I'm jealous as fuck.

What I ought to do is walk up to her right now and sweep her off her feet, taking her from the room and back to my bed where she belongs. But I distract myself with the conversation at the table, sneaking glances in her direction every now and then.

Until the moment that the key note speaker steps up onto the stage and talks about all the big donors for the night, one of which is my firm. I look over to her table and lock eyes with her. The look on her face goes from wide-eyed shock to confusion, to something resembling embarrassment as her cheeks go pink and she sits up straight, noticeably shifting away from her date. I smirk and her eyes narrow as she realizes that I've obviously been watching her for a while. I nod a silent hello before shifting my attention back to the speaker, not looking back at her for the duration of the speech.

It's not until after the dinner, when the band starts playing and couples start congregating on the dance floor, that I decide it's time to make my next move. Waiting until Tanner is engaged in what looks like deep conversation with the man next to him, I stand and move toward Samantha's table.

"Samantha, what a surprise to see you again." I purposefully pause to take in how breathtaking she looks in close quarters. She's wearing a demurely sexy, black V-neck dress. Standing above her I get a glimpse of a black lace bra that has my dick twitching in anticipation of seeing more, but I try to calm my thoughts and clear my head, focusing on the end game—getting my girl back.

"Y-Yes. Hi, Sean. Fancy seeing you here …" she says, leaving her comment open ended in anticipation of an answer.

"Yes, a funny coincidence, wouldn't you say? Fortunately, my boss called in a favor late this afternoon and I'm attending the dinner in his place."

"I see." She fidgets in her seat and curls her hair back behind her ear repeatedly. Her apparent nervousness is very becoming.

"Babe, who's this?" The dickhead to her left asks, unapologetic as he turns toward me, obviously sizing me up. His words are clipped, his tone aggressive at best.

"Tanner, this is Sean Miller. He's an old friend of mine," Sam says, emphasizing the word friend. Her eyes sparkle with amusement as I hold my hand out to Tanner who just looks at it before slowly shaking. A firm but inconspicuous squeeze gives his true thoughts away, making the smile on my face morph into a knowing grin.

"Great to meet you, Tanner. I wasn't aware Samantha was seeing anyone—"

"I'm not!" she interjects harshly, not realizing how much she has just given away. She looks at him quickly with guilt written all over her face before turning back toward me. "I mean, Tanner and I are just friends and colleagues."

My grin gets bigger at her unintentional admission. "Great, then you won't mind me stealing Samantha away for a dance. We have a lot of catching up to do, don't we, friend?"

Her lips twitch as she tries to hold back a smile, recognizing a pissing contest when she sees one. "Yes, we do. You don't mind, do you, Tanner?"

"Nope, go ahead," he grumbles as he picks up his glass and knocks it back quickly. "I'm going to get another drink."

"Fantastic," I boast before holding out my hand to my dance partner, and wrapping my fingers around hers as she places it in mine. She pushes her chair out before standing radiantly in front of me.

"After you …" I offer, gesturing for her to lead the way. I'm not used to doing the following and I know she realizes that this is not the norm. To her credit, she doesn't hesitate as she walks toward the dance floor, pulling me behind her.

She stops in the middle of the crowd of swaying couples, turning to look at me. I swear if that woman cocks her hip and glares at me expectantly, I won't be able to stop myself from doing something highly inappropriate for a police charity dinner. Instead, she bites her lip and steps into my arms as I hold them out in front of me. Pulling her in close against me, I gently place my right hand on her left hip. Lacing her other hand's fingers with mine, I hold our hands up as I start to sway side to side in time to I Hate The Way I Love You by Rihanna and Ne-Yo.

She leans into me, her body relaxing into mine as if it's the most natural thing in the world for us to be dancing together. Taking her lead, I glide my hand up her back until it rests across her shoulders. A contented sigh escapes her lips and I will my body to control itself as I feel an all too familiar tightness in my groin. Something about this woman obliterates all semblance of the control I pride myself on. It should worry me, but then again it was always like this with Sammy. Everything felt right, natural, like we belonged.

"What are we doing, Sean?" she whispers quietly. She looks up at me and her big jade eyes hit me like a sucker punch. "Because I'm not sure I can resist for much longer ..." she murmurs, her voice tapering off as if she's unsure of what she's saying.

"Why resist?" I murmur as I rest my cheek against her hair.

"You know why. We don't work."

"Hmm ..." I say, continuing to move against her, not stopping as the song ends and the lead singer starts playing Coldplay's I Ran Away.

She drops her head to my shoulder, and the contentment I feel from holding her in my arms consumes me. Her arm strokes my back, making my muscles flex at the sensation. I can feel the heat from her touch through my suit jacket, and I can't focus on anything other than the beautiful woman in my arms. This is so damn right. I don't know how she can keep me at arm's length but she's worth the wait. Everything in me wants to whisk her away, show her how good we were, how good we can be.

After a few minutes, the song comes to an end and the MC announces that the band will be taking a short break. As if waking from a trance, I move my arms away from her and gently push her away from my body.

"Sean, what's wrong?"

Her eyes dart around the room, looking over my shoulder toward her table where I know her dickhead date will be watching her like a hawk. Friends with benefits my ass! One look at him with her and I knew he wanted more than just benefits; he wants the whole damn package. Pity I can't let that happen. Ever. "Thank you for the dance, Samantha. I got carried away there for a minute and forgot myself."

She looks up at me, her eyebrows furrow in confusion at my sudden change. "Did I … Did I do something wrong?" she stutters.

"No, it was all me. I must be going, I've got to go check in at the club." I grab her hand and lift it to my mouth, gently kissing the back of it before letting it go. "Nice seeing you again, Sammy."

I muster all the restraint I have and turn around, walking away from the one woman I never want to leave, the one who needs to make a decision about what and who she truly wants.

And soon.

Sam

I stand in the middle of the dance floor watching Sean's back as he walks away from me, again. I feel embarrassed, turned on and frustrated as hell, and I have to lock my knees to stay upright.

Being in Sean's arms again felt better than I remembered. It was like the world around us disappeared and we were the only two people left. I can still feel where Sean's hands touched my hip, up my back, across my shoulders, my cheek where I laid my head on his shoulder, my chest where it was pressed snugly against his …

I stumble to the bar and order a vodka tonic—more vodka, less tonic—then down it in one gulp before ordering another one, seeking anything that will clear my head.

When I reach my table again, Tanner and Zander are deep in conversation.

"Sam!" Kate calls as I sit down in my seat. "We were just saying how we should head out to a club. It's only nine o'clock, way too early to be calling it a night. You up for it?"

Tanner looks over at me and raises a brow, anticipating my normal polite decline. Bolstered by the alcohol coursing through me, I suddenly feel full of energy and ready to dance.

Fuck it! Sean walked away and left me all worked up and confused as hell. Who says we can't go to his fucking club and give him a taste of his own medicine? How dare he approach me in front of my colleagues and friends and get all possessive in front of Tanner, not trying to hide how jealous he obviously was, then dance with me. AND he didn't just dance like an old pair of friends; he danced with me like he was my man, my lover … branding me and igniting my body with his touch.

How fucking dare he!

"That's an awesome idea!" I exclaim, standing up and grabbing Tanner's hand, wobbling slightly on my heels before he cups my shoulders to steady me.

"You okay, babe?" he asks, sounding concerned.

"Sure, let's do this. I know just the club."

I lead Tanner outside the club, Kate and Zander bringing up the rear. I start walking down the street, hand in hand with Tanner as I try hard to ignore the fact that I feel nothing toward him. No spark, no warmth spreading through my body, no fluttering in my belly like when Sean is near. I know I'm probably leading him on, but right now I have one thing on my mind and that is showing Sean exactly what he's missing, exactly what he walked away from.

"Where are we headed, Sam?" Zander asks, coming up beside me.

I don't hesitate. I don't even look up at him as I answer. I just keep striding toward my destination. The desire to see Sean again is all the motivation I need to walk three blocks in four inch pumps as I decree, "We're going to Throb. We're going to get drunk and have some fun."

Drunk woman on a mission.

Get the fuck out of my way.

CHAPTER 13: "YOU GOT THE LOVE"

Sam

I scan the club hoping to catch a glimpse of the man that I can't stop thinking about.

I've been secretly hoping that Sean is watching me on the dance floor and will sweep me out of Tanner's arms into his. Wishful thinking obviously. I can't sort my head out. I know I want him, but I keep waiting for him to make his move and he hasn't tried to seal the deal yet. He gets so far then pulls back, leaving me hot and bothered and aching for more.

One could almost think he wants me to go to him!

As soon as we walk in the doors of the club, I make a beeline for the bar and order a round of shots. Tanner then follows suit, ordering another round, and before too long my overactive mind has blurred edges and I'm feeling relaxed and carefree. But even in my tipsy state, I can't get Sean out of my head.

He was so overtly possessive earlier in front of Tanner. And when he held me in his arms as we danced, the energy between us was electric. I mean, if there was ever a power crisis, just put Sean and me in a small room together and watch the kilowatts go through the roof!

My skin prickles with awareness and I instantly know he is nearby. No other man has made me so on edge. There is no one else on earth that I've ever felt this in tune with before; it's disconcerting and thrilling at the same time.

Pony by Rihanna blasts through the sound system and Tanner takes the opportunity to move in close, hooking his arm around my waist and pulling me hard against him. The dance floor fills to bristling, but the people are a blur. All I can feel is Tanner's hard body writhing suggestively in time with the music and the all too familiar buzz in my head from too much vodka. My body is strung so tight I fear I'll snap, and it's that pent-up tension that sees me matching Tanner grind for grind, my hips swinging seductively with his as I lift my arms around his neck, tangling my hands in his hair and pulling the strands through my fingers. I close my eyes and for a moment I imagine it's Sean I'm dancing with, that it's his hands wandering over my body, the silky material of my dress sliding up slightly when one hand rakes against the bare skin of my thigh while the other cups my ass, holding me tight against him. I reopen my eyes as Tanner's hands glide over me, remaining oblivious to the discomfort I feel the minute I lock eyes with Sean.

His sapphire eyes bore into mine from across the crowded club as he leans against the stairs on the far wall that lead up to the second floor and his office; the office where he'd told me I could find him if I needed him.

In my heart, I know I don't want Tanner; it was never an emotional connection with him. Don't get me wrong, he's a really nice guy, but he's not him. When I think about it, nobody has even come close to him. My resolve to fight whatever feelings still rage between us is failing. Those deep blue eyes, that knowing smirk of his that tells me he's thinking dirty thoughts and they all involve me, the way his touch relaxes and charges me all at the same time. My automatic supplication whenever he's near.

I haven't been able to admit that to myself until right now when I'm in the arms of another man, and in a club with an illicit reputation that both scares and exhilarates me as I stare into the eyes of the man who makes my heart race like no other.

Tanner and I continue to dance as Rihanna talks about doing it, but it's the rest of the words that sink into my psyche about having a lover and needing no other.

Sean's head tilts upward, his chin strong and unwavering. Even from across the room I can see that he's tense, his rigid body unmoving, his jaw clenched so tightly that if I were closer I'd swear I could hear his teeth grinding. Frowning and shaking his head, he turns and speaks to the bouncer briefly before taking the stairs two at a time, striding away from me, away from us. Tanner buries his face in my neck, and when I feel his tongue on my skin I realize why Sean left.

I feel like I've been sucker punched in the gut.

I need to go to him, I need to show him that I want this, want him. Not Tanner.

"Sam," A voice whispers in my ear, bringing me out of my haze. "You wanna get out of here? Any more of this…" Tanner murmurs as he grinds his hard length against me, "…and I'll get arrested, even in a club with a perverted reputation like this."

His words act like cold water. Pulling away, I take a step back while pushing on his shoulders to put a decent gap between us. His eyes narrow as he frowns down at me. "Sam, what's wrong?" His hands covertly go into his pockets as he tries to hide his predicament. If I were in the right frame of mind I'd find it amusing, but right now nothing is funny. It's like I've just been hit with a Mac truck of realization and there is only one man I want to see standing in front of me. The one man who I know is probably still watching this situation unfold, that's if he hasn't washed his hands of me. Seeing me in the arms of another man in front of him would do that. I know that the mere thought of Sean being with another woman, let alone touching her, kills me.

I can't deny this anymore. He knows me, he knows the real me, and the man still makes my days brighter, my dreams hotter, and can command a room like he owns the joint. He's strong, he's dedicated, and hard working. In fact, he's turned out to be everything he promised me he would be—successful, committed, and willing to build a life for us.

And I never gave him a chance.

What am I? Fucking stupid or what! I had a man ready to give me the world and I walked away.

I shake my head as Tanner puts his hand on my bare arm. His touch doesn't warm me like it used to.

"Look, Tan, I'm sorry."

"You're sorry?" He looks at me in utter disbelief. "For what? Getting me worked up in a club? 'Cause baby, as long as you help me work my way down, all is forgiven."

"No. I'm sorry because I can't do this with you anymore."

"This?" He waves his hand between us and I nod. He stares at me for a moment, two of us standing in a throng of unaware dancers continuing to shift around us.

I drop my head to the floor, my shoulders slumping in defeat as I refuse to register the hurt in his eyes. I look up to see Tanner's back as he walks away from me toward the club's front door. Once he disappears from sight, my eyes move to the stairs leading up to where Sean is, the man I truly want. My feet are stuck and I'm standing there motionless in a mass sea of flying limbs and sweaty bodies, caught between what my heart and body want and what my mind is telling me I'm not in a position to handle.

One heel in front of the other … one step at a time, I make my way to the stairs. The bouncer holds his hand up to stop me and as I open my mouth to tell him who I want to see. He tilts his head toward his earpiece, his eyes cutting to me. With a chin lift, he steps aside. "Last door on the left, Samantha."

My head snaps up to his at the sound of my name. Sean knows I'm coming. He's been watching me which means he saw me stop Tanner and then saw Tanner leave the club. My stomach fills with butterflies as I climb the stairs. To the left is a private bar that Sean told me was for members to use away from the general public, either before or after they'd partaken in the VIP rooms. I turn to the right and see a dimly lit hallway lined with low hanging red tinted lamps, and heavy wooden doors line each side of the walls with colors fading from black to scorching hot red.

When I reach the very end of the corridor, I pause for a moment, resting my head against the cool wood as I try to collect my thoughts and prepare myself for whatever might happen in the office I'm about to enter. Will he be angry? Or will he be eerily calm in a way that is all Sean?

I stand up straight, looking down my body to check that I'm presentable before pushing my hair back behind my ears and knocking once firmly, then softer a second time as my momentary bravado starts to lose steam.

A few seconds later, the door opens and my vision is filled with Sean—shirt loose and unbuttoned at the top, his eyes tight, his expression indiscernible.

"Samantha," he murmurs, not taking his eyes away from my face which is telling.

"Can I come in?"

"Do you want to? Or are you just in need of a ride home? I just watched your friend leave alone," he sneers.

"Sean, please. We need to talk."

He steps aside and I walk past him, the small space forcing me to turn sideways as I brush past him. My breasts graze his chest and I gasp as sparks ignite between us. I slowly look back up at him and see his stormy eyes full of heat, so I quickly step into his office and stop in the middle of the room, turning around to face him. I'm not feeling as drunk as I did downstairs. The importance of the next few minutes acts like the most potent cup of coffee I could ever drink.

He shuts the door, turning the lock before facing me and leaning back against the door. His head drops and he takes me in, starting at my black strappy heels up my legs and working his way slowly over my curves. His intense gaze feels like a gentle caress full of heat and promise. I shudder and I know he doesn't miss it. I'm so turned on right now that I swear he could breathe on me and I'd climax instantly. It feels right to be with him. Despite my misconceptions about his strength and his power over me, Sean is the most in control man I have ever known.

So why am I shaking like a leaf in anticipation?

Sean

"I shouldn't want this," she murmurs quietly, unsure of what she is saying. I watch her body, looking for cues to prove what I already know. She's lying to herself and more importantly, to me.

Staying grounded where I am, my back to the office door, I watch her face and the inner battle ensuing between the need to stay and the desire to run. And it is a need; even if she hasn't realized it yet. "But you need it, Samantha. You need me, don't you?"

I take a step toward her as she steps back until her body hits my desk. I continue to advance and her chest rises and falls quickly, her breathing labored as her body tells me what she is not yet prepared to admit.

When I stop the heat from her body radiates through mine, and I have to stifle a groan at the sheer magnetism of the woman in front of me. Her untapped compliance that she still refuses to acknowledge after all of these years draws me in.

Closing my eyes I stand and simply breathe her in. Her coconut scent, the same body lotion she used to use back in college, brings back memories of our bodies entwined, our lips meshed together as I brought her to climax time and time again. I shake my head and open my eyes, meeting hers full of latent heat and desire.

"Sean, I—"

No. She's not getting another moment to talk herself out of this, out of us. She's been running for way too long. This time, it's for keeps. This time, I'm not letting anything come between us. Not her mother. Not my brother. Not her job. Not some convoluted idea she gets in her head that she is not the submissive I need her to be. I'm sick of the bullshit and this time, I want what is mine. And Sam is mine.

Wrapping my arm around her waist, I pull her body tight against mine and slant my head, slamming my mouth to hers as she gasps in shock. My hand grabs her blonde ponytail, holding her in place, and her tight muscles relax as soon as my tongue rolls over hers.

I set out to rediscover the beauty that is Samantha Richards.

Her taste is intoxicating and I find myself wanting to consume her, to lose myself inside of this gorgeous woman whose mind continues to deny the never-ending connection between us. In this moment, I want to show her everything I am, everything I can do to her, every possible way I can make her feel. I know I'm losing control, but with Sam ...

I don't care.

I press my hips into her, pressing my hard-as-steel cock against the softness of her stomach. I feel her arms move between us, and when I expect her to push her palms against my chest and push me away, she fists my shirt and pulls me closer, thrusting her hips into me in silent invitation. She may not be able to admit the words, but she can show me with her body, with her actions. She can no longer deny that the spark between us is as strong as it was in the beginning.

I pull my head back slightly, raking my teeth against her bottom lip as I go. I scan her face, looking for any remaining uncertainty. But all I can see are swollen pink lips and eyes full of want and I know in that moment that I have my Sammy back, even if it's just for a few moments, a few hours, maybe a night. And if that is all I get with her, then I'll take it willingly. If this is the only chance I have, I'm going to make it count. I'm going to draw it out and make it last until neither one of us can move. Hell, until neither of us can breathe without remembering the way we were and this night.

"You were saying?" I say, raising an eyebrow.

"Don't stop," she rasps, then she shocks the hell out of me by cupping my cheeks with her warm, velvet soft hands and guiding her mouth back toward mine. Slow, tentative licks with her tongue against my lips remind me that as much as I want this woman, my Sam, I need to start slow and work her up to my level. The same level where I believe she wants to be, where she'll be hoarse from screaming out my name as she comes over and over again. Fuck, I want that.

I give her a few minutes, letting her have some semblance of control before I take over again. Forceful, demanding Sean is back in the room. I'm not going to ask anymore, I'm going to take what I want. And right now, I want my Sammy to be writhing breathless beneath me as I take her. I feel any leftover resistance seep from her body as she relaxes against me, tacit acceptance of everything I'm giving her and more. I tilt my head and plunder her mouth, my hand on her waist slipping down to her ass, my fingers gripping tightly, making her feel every inch of what is waiting for her. My other hand grips her hair roughly, pulling just enough to demand her attention. Her answering moan is all the fuel I need as I drag my mouth along her jaw and down her neck, nipping with my teeth before soothing with a lick of my tongue. I move my leg between hers, lifting my thigh until it's flush against her warm center, angling her pelvis hard against my leg with pressure on her ass until Sam's instincts take over and her hips start thrusting against my leg, seeking the friction she needs to find exquisite pleasure she seeks, the ecstasy I want to give her.

"Fuck," she moans as I continue to kiss her neck. I can't get enough of her; I never want to stop. Her skin tastes divine, exactly how I remember, sweet as honey and sexy as sin.

She tastes like home.

She continues to grind against my thigh, my throbbing cock straining against her hip, hard as steel and likely to leave bruises by morning, but right now I want more from her, need more. Releasing my grip on her hair, I trail my palm down the back of her neck, running my fingers over the curve of her shoulder and down inside the V of her dress. Slipping my fingers inside the satin cup of her bra, I curl my hand around the curve of her breast, gently squeezing in time with the thrust of her hips against me. I swipe my thumb across her hard nipple, loving the shudder that surges through her body. Her breathing quickens, letting me know how close she is to coming.

Leaning forward, I nip her earlobe. "Come for me, Sammy. Let me hear you cry out my name."

"Holy shit!" she screams as her climax hits her and she rides it out with hard and long strokes of her pelvis against my leg. It takes every ounce of control I have to stop myself from coming in my pants like a horny teenager.

I move my hand out of her top and start running my hands slowly over her back and arms as she comes down from her extraordinary high. That was sexy as shit and I can't wait to feel her come all around my cock. I pull my leg away, smiling when I hear her mournful whimper at the loss.

"Sammy, I need more than this. Let me show you how good it can be. Give me this. Tonight." I cup her jaw with my hands, my eyes boring into hers as I wait for her answer. I hold my breath because I don't know what I'll do if she pulls away from me again. It hurt the first time, and even big bad Doms aren't invincible. Twice would shatter me.

Her breath fans over my face as she struggles to recover. Her eyes drop to my mouth, then back up to meet mine. She nods as her lips part, and I watch as her tongue darts out to touch her swollen mouth. "But not here. I want you, Sean, but I can't do it here. I just can't."

I watch her for a few seconds, realizing that she's being completely upfront with me. Her hands resting on my hips haven't moved, and she hasn't pulled her body away from mine. She's fully on board with the idea of this, of us, but as her head drops to the floor I realize she's holding her breath too.

"Anything you want. This is about us. Not the club. Not our past. Nothing except you and me, here and now. I've never wanted anybody as much as I want you." I reach down and adjust myself in my slacks. My cock is so hard it hurts. It's been a long time that I've felt like this. "I want you to know, I never play at home, only here. You're the only woman I want in my bed right now." I shut my mouth suddenly, stopping myself from saying that if I had my way, she'd be the last too. Baby steps, Miller. I've waited for her to come to me, now I have to bide my time.

"Sean, I—"

"No. Don't tarnish this with regret or apologies, Sam. If you're sure about this," I take a step back and hold out my hand toward her, "then take a chance on me, on us. I want to show you how good we can be. I want to have a chance to prove to you that we're good together."

Without any hesitation, she places her hand in mine, forcing me to bite back a smirk of satisfaction. I give her hand a gentle squeeze of encouragement before pulling her hard into my chest. Reverently kissing her temple, I hold my lips against her skin. "You're not going to regret this."

"I know" she whispers. "Believe me, I know."

CHAPTER 14: "BREATHE (2AM)"

Sean

Lying on my back in my third floor master bedroom, I stare at the ceiling as sleep evades me. Looking to my bedside table, I see the time tick over to 2 a.m. but I don't care. It's the early hours of Sunday morning, and the woman I could never get enough of is asleep in my arms, her head resting in the crook of my shoulder, her naked leg tangled with mine with her hand resting on top of my chest, directly above my heart.

It shouldn't feel so right, should it? Whatever this is between Sammy and I shouldn't feel so good right off the bat, like there was never a decade we lost.

My plans to bring her back to the condo and reconnect with her in the most pleasurable physical way were curtailed when Sam fell asleep on my shoulder in the car on the way home. I wasn't pissed off though; she was still slightly drunk and sleepy in her adorable post-orgasmic haze. When we arrived at my door, I carried her up the stairs and into my bedroom, laying her down on the bed.

"Can't sleep in clothes," she murmured as she clumsily tried to take her dress off over her head without standing up, all the while mumbling, "Sleep naked," to me.

"Just wait, Sammy, I'll help you."

"You just want me naked and begging." Her husky, slurred voice pulled at me.

I leaned in close, dragging my large hands over her hips and dragging the soft material of her dress up with them, making sure to feel the smooth expanse of her skin under my touch. I didn't miss the small shudders or the goose bumps that followed, and I had to bite back a groan when she arched her back subconsciously and thrust her breasts even closer to my face.

That wasn't my only problem.

1) There was a half-naked Sammy lying on my bed, in my house, the two of us alone in private and void of interruptions for the next eight hours at least.

2) She was being sexy and funny and cute and I didn't want to do a thing about it until she was awake, sober and cute.

3) My black cotton boxers covering her smooth pussy kept taunting me. It was hard enough keeping my hands to myself when I saw what lay underneath after she insisted I change her underwear.

4) The glimpse of her breasts through her black lace bra was begging me to put my mouth on her.

My night had gone south when I saw that cretin pawing at her in my club. When she saw me, I didn't miss the flash of guilt that washed over her features. I could tell she was thinking of me, imagining … no, wishing it were me with her, touching her, kissing her.

Don't get me wrong, I'm all for a bit of exhibitionism in the right context, but watching the woman I want, the woman I need, get dry humped in front of me is not my thing, so I mentioned to my bouncer that Sam was allowed up if she approached him, but no one else, and that I'd be in my office if anyone needed me. The hardest thing out of all of that was turning my back on her and walking away.

But walking away from each other seems to be a bad habit of ours, doesn't it?

I managed to dress her in one of my T-shirts, and my boxers so that her dignity remained intact. Once she was sleeping soundly on her side in my bed, I stripped off and walked into my en suite and turned the shower on, not bothering to close the door. Not waiting for the water to warm up, I was immediately hit with cold water from all six jets, soaking me from all directions. Feeling my built-up lust ease slightly along with the stresses of the night, I finally started to relax, but my cock still ached for relief. I swear, I was in physical pain from being turned on for too long.

I resisted the temptation to take matters into my own hands in the shower and stepped out, drying myself off before returning to the bedroom and dropping the towel around my waist, hopping into bed next to her.

I turn my head to the side and watch the slow rise and fall of her chest. I wonder if she'll change her mind in the light of day; whether she'll bolster her defenses and close herself off again. Fuck, I hope not. I'll just have to distract her so that it doesn't happen.

There is something about having a naked woman in my bed wearing something of mine that fills me. She's actually here, back in my life and my bed. If you'd asked me a month ago whether I thought that it would be possible, I would have laughed at you and told you to take a hike.

Turning onto my back, I put my arm behind my head. 2 a.m. and I'm home, in bed, with a beautiful woman. This is unheard of, but hell if I don't like it. A lot. The only thing to make it better would be for her to be naked and awake, writhing beneath me.

She rolls toward me, tangling her legs with mine and plastering her body against mine as she rests her hand on my chest, directly above my heart. Fuck! That instantly gets my cock standing to attention again. Just when I thought I'd be able to make it until morning.

Reaching down with my left hand, I squeeze my cock hard, willing the fucker to settle down and let me sleep. Instead, just touching the hard shaft hardens me further. Sammy's leg moves against mine, the smooth skin slowly sliding down, then back up again. I look down at her and her eyes are still closed, her hand on my chest remains motionless. Still asleep.

Out of habit, my hand fists my dick and I give in to temptation and give myself a few very welcome strokes. Fuck, it feels good. I feel her fingers twitch which just spurs me on. I tighten my grip and stroke slowly down and then back up, biting back a groan when her leg repeats its torturous trip down and back up again.

I should stop right now, but with Sammy half on me and her leg mirroring the movements on my cock, that seems near impossible.

Another stroke, another shot of pleasure shoots through me.

Just when I'm looking down at my fist as it palms my cock, Sammy's hand slowly drifts down my chest, her index finger tracing the lines of my abs until her hand wraps around mine and she moves our hands over my length, up and down, slowly increasing the speed. She squeezes her hand around mine and this time I don't bother hiding my satisfaction, swearing softly under my breath as I watch us, captivated by the sight of our joined hands stroking my eager dick. I move my hand on top of hers and direct her, the first touch of her soft skin on me sending a surge of total satisfaction through my body.

I turn my head and her bright green eyes burn into mine. She leans her head until our mouths are almost touching, our hands never stopping their assault as she traces the seam of my lips with her tongue. I growl and attack her mouth with renewed hunger, our tongues entwining and our hands speed up.

Stroking up and down as my tongue rolls over hers, our lips glued together as we breathe heavily, my climax rushing through me like a stampede.

"Fuck, Sammy, don't stop," I mutter as she pulls away and starts kissing my neck while tightening her grip and silently willing me to finish what I started.

"Fuck, Sammy!" I roar as I climax, our hands still moving as I spill onto my stomach.

I turn my head and take her mouth, murmuring words of appreciation and awe between kisses.

Well, fuck me, the woman isn't backing off.

And fuck if I'm not looking forward to taking her again.

Sam

I open my eyes to the wide, hard expanse of Sean's chest under me. His chest rises and falls softly as he sleeps soundly, and the overwhelming sense of comfort I feel surges through me.

I did it. It wasn't a dream last night when I gave up fighting and went to his office, giving myself to this man who has been invading my thoughts and feelings for the past few weeks. I shift my body slightly, feeling his arm resting gently on my bare hip, my leg lying on top of his like it is just another morning, an everyday occurrence. My hand is positioned on top of his heart, the steady staccato beat vibrating through my fingers. His smooth, warm skin calls for me to run my hand over him, to explore his hard sculpted body once again.

"Good morning," he huskily murmurs from above. I jerk my head up and meet his half open blue eyes that are filled with heat, immediately igniting my desire for this gorgeous man.

I smile up at him. "Morning."

"How are you feeling?" he asks, lifting his arms across his body and smoothing my wayward hair off my face.

"I'm good," I whisper as I give in to temptation and flex my fingers against him. "It wasn't a dream."

His lips tip up. "No, Sammy. Definitely not a dream. No regrets?"

"None. Well, maybe one …"

His brows lift up in surprise. "One?"

I softly laugh at his reaction. He's obviously thinking the worst. "No, not this. Not at all. It was probably the easiest decision I've made in a long time. I'm just sorry that I fell asleep last night …"

"Well, now that we can make up for." He cups my cheek with his hand and lowers his mouth, slowly kissing my lips, his tongue making gentle languid strokes against mine as my body melts into his. Lifting my leg higher, I brush my thigh against his hard cock and my pussy tightens in anticipation. He groans into my mouth as our kiss amps up, my tongue submitting to his as his fingers dig into my hips, his palm hardening against my jaw as he attacks my mouth with renewed hunger. I pull away slightly from his mouth, now panting as my hips instinctively rock against his side.

"I need to be inside you, Sammy, more than I need my next breath. I need to make love to you, assure myself that you're really here with me, in my bed." His hand trails down my neck, moving down to my breast as he cups its weight and runs his thumb across my hard nipple. "I need you … to feel your thighs clench around my shoulders as I taste you. I need to feel your pussy clench around my cock as I enter you again, I need to make every inch of your body mine … to make you come hard around me. I want to hear you cry out my name as I move inside you."

Fuck! I need that and more. "Yes, I want you. Make my body yours again, Sean."

"With fucking pleasure, darling."

I whip his tee off my body before he swiftly rolls over me, laying his hard body on top of mine, and my thighs which instantly open to accommodate his stiff cock. He kisses me hard and fast again, his tongue exploring my mouth with a hunger that I've craved for way too long. He completely overtakes me with his ravenous hunger, tasting and taking my mouth with a heat I've only been able to dream about. He shifts his body lower and peppers my neck with open mouthed kisses, nipping gently, then soothing with a swirl of his tongue moving down again, taking a pebbled nipple in his mouth while his hand gently squeezes the other breast. I moan with pleasure as electric pulses run directly down to my pussy, its slick wetness preparing me for his most welcome invasion.

"Sean," I moan as he looks up at me through hooded eyes, placing more kisses as his mouth travels lower over my stomach until he is head height with my pulsing clit. Hooking his fingers underneath the waistband of the boxers I'm wearing, he slowly drags them down my thighs before throwing them over his shoulder and slowly gliding his hands back up until I'm a writhing mess, panting embarrassingly as he spreads my thighs wide then moves his thumbs to open me as he takes in my bare lady garden. With a sly grin and his eyes locked with mine, he darts his tongue out and circles my clit, sending a full body shudder through me.

My hands automatically grab his head, my fingers tangling in his hair and firmly holding him against me. "Un-uh," he says, wrapping his hands around my wrists and pulling them to the bed, holding them firmly in place as he continues to lap at me, circling and sucking, licking me end to end as my body sings with desire. My heart races, knowing that I have to take whatever he gives me, feel whatever he wants me to feel. My belly tightens as my climax rushes me, and the moment Sean wraps his lips around my clit and sucks hard, I shatter into a million pieces.

"Sean! Shit! Fuck! Oh, my godddddd!" I scream as my back arches, my hips holding firm against his mouth. He gently eases back and softly licks my slit backward and forward, the sensation drawing out the waves of ecstasy as I return to earth. I'm in a haze as he moves up my body, dragging his weight against me as I feel his smooth steel cock inch closer to my core.

He kisses my lips and moves my hands up the side of our bodies and over my head, never letting go as he secures them in one of his own. The sweet taste of my come on his lips spins me into a frenzy as I wrap my legs around his hips, and pull his body hard against mine. I moan as he runs his hard length against me

"Pleaaasssseeee …" I groan.

"Shit!" he curses as he rests his head against my forehead and stills his torturous movements.

Unable to touch him with my hands, I lift my chin to kiss his jaw tenderly. "What's wrong? Don't stop."

He lifts his head and looks straight at me, his eyes still dark with lust but also soft and gentle. "I've got no protection here. It's downstairs in my wallet." I swear he blushes with embarrassment. My big bad Dom embarrassed? Never thought I'd see the day. He goes to get off me and I wrap my legs around his hips, pinning him in place and start giggling.

After staring at me in disbelief, his grimace turns into a smirk. "What are you laughing at?"

It takes a few moments to compose myself. "I've got an implant, and I always use condoms, but I trust you, Sean …" I look up at him, my expression turning serious as I realize how big of a step this is. This is the most vulnerable I have been with him, the most open, trusting, and willing. He nods once and lowers his body, bringing his lips back to mine, keeping his eyes wide open as he lovingly explores with his tongue, nipping my bottom lip before sucking it into his mouth.

His hard cock probes my entrance, and I instinctively open my legs wider, inviting him inside me. It's an invitation he doesn't need. With my wrists bound above my head, his lips meshed with mine, he slowly inches his way inside me, my walls clinging to him tightly. "Fuck me, Sammy. You feel incredible. I need to move." Totally speechless, all I can do is lift my hips to thrust against him, encouraging him to make love to me.

Our hips move rhythmically against each other as he sets a slow and torturous pace, stoking the raging inferno inside me that has been threatening to explode ever since I woke up.

"Grab the headboard, Sammy. Hold on and don't let go," he orders, his voice a low growl. His grip on my wrists loosen and I stretch out my fingers, wrapping them around the thick wooden slats of his headboard, bucking against him as he continues to pump inside me. The thrill I feel at making him lose control heightens my pleasure. Knowing that my submission is the same gift to him as his dominance is giving me lifts me higher than I've ever felt before. I groan as he sucks hard on the delicate skin at the base of my neck. I know I'll have the hickey from hell there now, but all I want is Sean to lose control. I want him to go off the deep end and give me a sign that he is just as worked up as me right now because I'm seconds from detonating again.

"I'm close … shit, fuck, I'm close," I pant in his ear. "Sean, I need to …"

"Close your eyes. I want you to feel everything. My hard cock stroking inside you, my wet mouth on your skin, my sweaty body rubbing against yours. Feel me, Sammy. Feel everything and give it back to me."

And I do.

The minute I close my eyes, I can feel every warm inch of Sean as he worships my body. He's not just making love to me, he's consuming me, owning me, and I fucking love it.

"I want you to come, Sammy. I want you to come hard. I want to feel you squeeze my cock as I fill you. I need to feel you, Sammy. Fuck … come. Come now!"

He thrusts two more times, pounding into me before planting himself to the hilt and taking my mouth vigorously, groaning his release as I crash over the cliff, my orgasm surging through me as I tighten my limbs around him and enjoy the ride.

"Fuck, yes," he affirms as he rests his weight against my now spent body. "God, I missed you Sam. I missed you so fucking much."

When an intense, strong man, who usually keeps his feelings in check, expresses himself so clearly and so sure of himself, the woman who broke his heart and took her sweet ass time coming back to him listens. I let the words sink in as he rolls off me and tucks me into his side, running his hand up and down my skin soothingly. And for the first time in a long time, I know I've finally done the right thing.

I'm home.

CHAPTER 15: "GOODBYE, MY LOVER"

Sean

"So do I need to tie you to the bed while I go to the bathroom?"

Her eyes go wide, but I don't miss the flash of heat my threat has evoked. "No … why would you?" Her brows furrow and the look of confusion is adorable on her.

I lean down and plant a soft kiss at the end of her button nose. "Well, I'm hoping you won't want to run away from me now that I've given you two orgasms for breakfast, but I can never tell with you." I wink and she hits my chest with her palm.

"Well, we could always shower together, you know. Then we'll be saving the planet and you won't have to worry about me doing a magic disappearing act on you." She laughs before jumping up off the mattress and walking into my bathroom, shutting the door behind her.

I lay there stunned.

First at the return of the fun, carefree Samantha who I originally fell in love.

Second at the site of her pert naked backside as she sashays her way to the bathroom.

"You've got five minutes before I'm coming in after you!" I call out, feeling my cock harden at the mere thought of having her again.

"Promises promises, Sir," she goads. That's all the motivation I need. I pull the covers back and leisurely make my way to the bathroom. I open the door, greeted with a waft of thick steam.

121

"You think you can hide in here?" I ask teasingly as I walk blindly to the shower room, holding out my hands at what would be her hip height and searching for her warm naked body in the makeshift fog.

"I thought you'd get off on the thrill of the chase."

"I'd chase you anywhere, Samantha Richards."

"I tried to resist and look how that turned out. I think I might just stay put and see how well your old body can keep up with me now that I'm in my sexual prime," she murmurs in my ear. Hooking my arm around her waist, I roll her in front of me, her back to my chest. Reaching up and tangling my hand in her hair, I tug her head to the side and bite the apex of her neck and collarbone. She releases a low, dick hardening whimper as I ease my teeth back and run the flat of my tongue over the bruised skin.

"You're going to pay for that comment."

"I'm counting on it," she replies, her husky voice giving away just how much she enjoyed being chased.

An hour and no hot water later, she paid for it three times. Once with my fingers, once with my mouth, and lastly as I pumped my cock into her from behind while her hands were pinned to the shower wall and she milked my orgasm from me.

After a quick trip back to her apartment to grab some clean clothes for Sam, we're now on our way to breakfast. When she told me she wasn't back on shift until tomorrow, I asked her to spend the day with me. We have a lot of time to catch up on, and a lot of miscommunications to clear up. In order to move forward, we need a clean slate. Oh, then there is the little issue of her mother's meddling from ten years ago to deal with.

I remember the day we broke up, still so clear in my mind.

She'd been avoiding me for a few days after I'd met her mom for the first time. Let me tell you, Debra Richards is one hard ass S.O.B. and the way she berated Sam grated me like you would not believe.

Both my parents and grandparents showered Ryan and me with love, supporting us as we strived to become our own person, follow our own paths and forge new ones where there weren't any. But Sammy ... she was given another perspective, one that her ball busting mother instilled in her, one which meant that under no circumstances should she let a man take care of her; that she should never rely on a man because heaven forbid she make the same mistakes Debra made.

After two days of Sam hiding away in her dorm room, I arranged for Helen to make herself scarce and knocked on their door with a bag of Chinese takeout, a bottle of vodka, and a smile. When Sam answered the door she looked a mess. Her hair was tied up on the top of her head in a messy bun, and she was wearing a loose fitting T-shirt two sizes too big with leggings. But she was still the most beautiful woman in the world.

Nothing seemed off about that night, even when I pushed her back onto her bed and stripped her clothing off, taking my time, binding her legs to the bed so that she was spread wide open for me. I made her scream my name until her voice was hoarse and cracking. And when I finally released her straining legs, she immediately wrapped them around my back and arched into me, lifting her breasts closer to my mouth as I rode out my climax.

We showered together and washed each other thoroughly before I fell asleep with her sleeping soundly in my arms like we had done so many times before. Had I known it would be the last time, I would have stayed awake, I would have made love to her one more time, made sure I left her with a lasting memory of us, one she couldn't have escaped from.

When I woke up, the bed was empty beside me. I looked around and saw Sam sitting on Helen's bed across the room from me.

"Beautiful, I like it better when I can feel you, not just see you."

She smiled softly, but her eyes said something else, something different. There were pain and heartache there, I just didn't understand it until she opened her mouth and said the words I never thought I'd hear from her. "I don't think is going to work, Sean." I watched in shock as she swallowed hard. "I think we're too different. Your need for control is too much for me. It's better to end it now before one of us gets hurt. I'm losing myself, my identity. College is such a short time in our lives, and I need to focus on graduating and immersing myself in the college experience. Being in a serious relationship doesn't help me do that."

I stared at her in shock. Standing up, I pulled my boxers and jeans up, then threw on my discarded shirt from the floor before stuffing my wallet in my pocket and walking toward her. "Sammy, I don't know where the hell this is coming from, but maybe you need some time to think. Seeing your mom has made you see things that simply aren't there …"

I reached out my hand to her, wanting to pull her up into my arms, but she looked up at me warily before standing of her own volition and walking around me, not even wanting to touch me. I can tell you, I felt that square in my chest.

"Fuck, Sammy. What the hell do you think you're trying to do? What happened between last night and this morning? I don't remember you complaining when you were sleeping in my arms. So why have you woken up sounding like a Debra Richards replica with an axe to grind against the male race?" I knew I should not have gotten angry, but I was confused as fuck and she was not explaining where all of it was coming from. She was saying things that could've been read straight out of her mother's hard ass playbook.

Sighing loudly, she walked to the door, pausing with her fist tightening around the handle. "It's for the best, Sean. I'm weaker when I'm with you.

124

You're getting ready to graduate. I've got my final year to finish. I think this is what … we need." The last few words were shaky at best. I knew that this was her mother's doing, but there was no reasoning with Sammy when she was this resolute about something.

Walking to the now open door, I stopped right in front of her, cupping her cheeks in both of my hands and lifting her face to mine. "I'm not giving up, Sammy. I don't understand this, but I know you. I know us. I know that there is more to us than just a college romance. You just need time. I love you, don't ever forget that." I brushed my lips gently against hers once, then again, and when I felt her body soften against mine, I slowly swept my tongue through her parted lips, making sure she felt my words deep inside, wanting her to feel everything I was trying to say in that one last kiss.

When I ended the kiss and walked away from her, I looked back once to see the door shutting quickly and my heart stuttered. But it wasn't until I walked into my house to find Ryan crying on the floor next to my grandfather's dead body that I knew what it was like to lose almost everything important in my life.

And when I went back to Samantha's dorm room to find her, to fight for her, at the time I needed her the most, she was gone.

Sam

Helen: Samantha Grace Richards, where the hell did you disappear to last night? Word is Tanner is pissed off and you were last seen going upstairs at Throb.

Me: Don't you full name me! I'm fine, more than fine. I'm with Sean …

Helen: OMG

A few minutes pass and then my phone vibrates again.

Rico: Be careful, minha amiga.

I chuckle to myself, earning a sideways glance from Sean as he squeezes my hand that is underneath his on the seat between us.

Me: So we're back to the double team text attack?

Helen: What do you expect?!? Girl, you better call me tonight and give me a full run down. I know the sex must have been out of this world!

Me: No comment.

Helen: Oh, come on. Give me something to get me through the day.

Rico: Please, for the love of God, give her something to shut her up ;)

I think for a moment. Do I really want to burst the Sean and Sam bubble just yet? I'd rather have an uninterrupted day to ourselves so that we can work out where we're going. On that, I send one last text.

Me: Last night was for me in his office, for him in bed, then for both of us this morning …

Rico: I think I like this guy already.

Rico: And you've succeeded in shutting Hels up, you're a legend. Have fun, talk tonight.

I turn my phone off and hand it to Sean, earning a quirked brow. "Don't give that back to me until tonight when I go home. I don't want any interruptions today." I smile at him and his eyes go soft as he lifts his hand and rests his palm on my cheek, giving me a gentle, probing, lazy kiss that I feel right down in my toes.

The butterflies in my stomach flutter once more as we head to breakfast. I know he's going to want to talk about our past, and to be honest, I'm prepared to go there if it means he can forgive me and move forward. I didn't miss the guarded approach he took with me this morning when we woke up. He was braced for me to bolt, but the thought didn't even cross my mind. I want him. I want everything he represents and offers. I want the man, the Dom, the lawyer, the whole damn package.

Whatever I need to deal with today to make him see that, bring it on.

CHAPTER 16: "RUN"

Sam

We've been in this out of the way café for half an hour now. Sean chose to sit next to me instead of opposite me and has been very tactile … touching my leg with his, brushing his arm against mine as he reaches for his coffee, and looking at me like he can't believe that I'm here. But there is still a slight hesitancy in his eyes. I hate that I'm the reason it's there and that, despite everything that happened between us last night and this morning, there is still a part of him expecting me to bolt.

I'm done with sacrificing my happiness for the sake of appearances. Trying to appear strong and independent while hungering for more has not been easy, but I did it. "I'm sorry," I blurt out, not wanting to wait another minute to get what is bound to be a difficult conversation out of the way. "I—"

He splutters into his coffee and looks at me. "Sammy, no …" I see shock, then resignation in his eyes and it cuts me to the core.

I quickly turn toward him, grabbing his hand and squeezing reassuringly. "Oh shit. No, Sean, I didn't mean … shit. I'm fucking this up." He furrows his brows and I know that I've totally confused him.

"I think you better spell it out for me because right now I'm thinking the worst. I'm expecting you to jump up and walk away from me … again."

"No, Sean, I'm not walking away. I want this, I want you." His lips curl up and his shoulders visibly relax. Thank God!

"About fucking time, Sammy," he says with a grin as he reaches up, smoothing my hair with his hand. "Because it was driving me insane watching you with that dickhead."

I snort loudly, then laugh. "Tanner is not a dickhead. He just wanted more than I wanted to give him, to give anyone who wasn't you."

He leans back, one arm resting on the back of my chair, the other cradling his coffee cup on the table. He's wearing a slim fitting white tee and jeans that cling to his butt and thighs like a stripper hugs her pole during happy hour. "So why did you stay away then? I left your bed and got home to find my grandfather dead on our living room floor. I called you. I came to find you."

I gasp. I didn't know he'd come back. All this time I thought he'd stayed away, that he didn't fight for me. "I ... I didn't know. I went straight to my mom's hotel room, then went back to Kentucky with her for a week to lick my wounds and nurse a broken heart."

His body goes rigid, and his fingers grip his cup tightly as his eyes go hard and cold. "Sorry and I hope you'll forgive me for saying this but that doesn't make it any less true. Your mother was a meddling, two-faced bitch who decided that I was no good for you after an hour of meeting me. Not knowing that I was so far gone for you I would've stayed strictly vanilla just to keep you in my bed and in my life. I loved you so damn much, Sammy. I had visions of our life together, of me practicing law and you being by my side as I built us an empire. You were it for me. Then the day I needed you most, I couldn't find you. I knew that it was to do with your mother, but you wouldn't talk to me. You shut me out and then cut me out of your life like I meant nothing. I may have been strong and confident, but you were my weak point. You were the one person who could obliterate me. And you did."

My eyes fill with tears as this beautiful dominant man in front of me bears his heart and soul.

"Sweetheart, I didn't want you to cry. I never tried to control you or dominate you … well, outside of the bedroom anyway." The corner of my mouth curls up as I remember just how true that was, and still is now. "I loved that you were strong and independent. That you didn't rely on me for anything even as much as I wanted you to. I just need you to understand where I was at. Why I have to know now whether you feel the same way?"

By the time I'd got back and found out about his grandfather's death, it was too late to pay my respects. I did send a card and some flowers to the house, but never heard anything. Then I saw him with another girl at a frat party and my heart sunk. That was when I decided to focus on school and friends and move on with my life, even though I knew that a piece of my heart had been lost.

"So why didn't you come back to me, Sammy? I got your card but you never called. I never saw you around campus, and then I graduated and our paths never crossed."

The million dollar question. Even after I realized my mother was wrong and that Sean wasn't my father, why didn't I fight for him? Try to win him back? "Stubborn pride? Stupidity? Jealously? Embarrassment? Take your pick." I shrug my shoulders, looking down because I'm too scared to look at him and see whatever emotion is swirling in his eyes staring back at me.

He leans over and puts his thumb under my chin, lifting my head up until our eyes meet. His gaze is unwavering as he studies my face. "Beautiful, I was waiting. I needed you and you weren't there. You disappeared and I couldn't talk to you. I would've taken you back in a heartbeat. Hell, if you'd told me in the hospital corridor that you were ready I would've stolen you away then and there."

My heart swells. Here I was thinking that Sean hated me, especially after I'd seen him with that other girl a few weeks after the break up. I thought I meant nothing to him and that my mother had been right all along.

"Jennifer Murray. You were with her at that frat party."

"She was Harry's new girlfriend. I was watching her back whenever he was elsewhere." He looks at me incredulously. "You thought I'd replace you just like that? We were together for a year, Sammy. Not once in that year had I even wanted to look at another woman."

"Oh," I mutter, feeling totally stupid. "You mean, I could've come to you, pleading, and we would've been together? If I hadn't listened to my mother and gone home with her? If I'd just stayed in my dorm room I would've seen you again?"

He stands up, pulling me with him and runs his arm up my spine, gently gripping my neck with his hand. His other hand cups my cheek as I take a sharp intake of breath. "If you had walked up to me at any time in the last ten years, Samantha Richards, I would've done exactly this …" His mouth is on me, hard and fast, claiming me, leaving no doubt as to the meaning behind it. I wrap my arms around his neck and respond fervently, moaning into his mouth in supplication as he continues to kiss the shit out of me. He's making sure that I get the message.

He wants me now, he wanted me back then, and by the feeling of his hard cock digging into my stomach, he wishes as much as I do that we weren't in the middle of a busy café right now.

Pulling away, I look at him, fully aware of the stupid, goofily happy grin on my face. "You finished breakfast?" I ask breathlessly, still recovering from that kiss of his that had me melting into a puddle on the floor.

"I'm suddenly hungry for something else. Should we take this party elsewhere?" he asks with that low, deep voice of his that calls to my insides, making my stomach flutter and my thighs clench.

"Fuck, yeah."

"I love that dirty mouth of yours," he mutters as he dumps some money on the table and leads me out the café's front door and toward his condo.

As soon as the door closes behind me, I'm pushed hard against the back of it. His hands slide into my hair and tug gently as he crashes his mouth down on mine and thrusts his tongue inside. My rigid body automatically relaxes under his touch, my hands gripping his shoulders as I struggle to match him stroke for stroke. My heart pounds in my chest and my nipples throb as he presses me even harder against the wooden door. He bends down slightly, pressing his stone hard cock against my clit as I moan loudly in his mouth.

"Fuck, I need to be inside you. I need to feel you on my cock as I fuck you senseless." His crude words send waves of lust through me as I stand there, pinned by his body, my hips taking on a life of their own as they rock back and forth against his cock. He trails his mouth down my neck, alternating between gentle scrapes of his teeth and firm sucking of my delicate skin. "Take me to bed, Sean."

"Abso-fucking-lutely."

He runs his hands down my back, hooking them under my ass and lifting me up. With nothing else to do, I wrap my legs around his waist and hold on as he effortlessly carries me up the stairs to the living room which is filled with bright sunlight, the wall of windows illuminating the room. "Screw the bed, I can't wait that long," he mutters as I bury my face in his neck, desperate to taste him in whatever way I can. He lays me down on the gray leather couch, holding me close as he glides his cock between my legs with hard, and purposefully slow, torturing thrusts. A reminder of what he's got and how much he knows I want it.

He slides down my body and kneels at my feet, throwing my shoes off, then undoing the fly of my jeans before gently pulling the denim down my legs. His change from rough to gentle muddles my brain as I struggle to keep up with the different sensations he's treating my body to. Suddenly, his mouth is on me, starting with my toes, then an open mouthed kiss on the arch of my foot, his hands caressing my skin as they move up my now parted legs. I close my eyes, trying to absorb the experience of Sean on his knees worshipping my body. I feel his warm breath on my shaking thighs as he grips my hips and trails his tongue along the crease of my hip, so close to where my body aches for him to be. He repeats himself on the other side, his hands holding my hips down as they threaten to buck up against him.

"Patience, Sammy. You know …"

His voice tapers off as he runs his nose down the length of my wet slit. Even through my underwear there is no way in hell he can't feel the damp material and smell just how much I'm aching for him. One of his hands moves, and with a growl and a rip, my panties are gone and Sean's tongue is buried deep inside me, his fingertips biting into my skin in a delicious contrast as he devours my pussy like a starved man.

"Fuck, Sean!" I cry out as he shifts his attention to my swollen clit and grates his teeth across the sensitive nerves, bringing my body to spasms as he sucks hard. My body is running head first into a mind-bending climax. I'm unable to speak as I fall flat on my back and trust that Sean will take care of me.

And he does.

His mouth lifts off me as two thick fingers spear inside of me. I moan in ecstasy as he pulls out and adds a third. "Fuck, I love your pussy, Sammy. So wet, so eager. You're gripping my fingers so tight. I can't wait to feel you grab hold of my cock." I'm a panting mess now, my breathing short and labored as I struggle to not come. Sean's hand grabs mine and strokes my clit with my outstretched finger.

"Take yourself there, Sammy. I want to watch you make yourself come while my tongue is buried deep in your pussy. Do it now, Sammy." Then his fingers are replaced with his tongue and I'm too far gone to care that I'm masturbating in front of this domineering man. I lift my head and meet his eyes which are watching my fingers rub my clit desperately, then I come—hard, screaming Sean's name like an epitaph as he licks and sucks my pussy, tasting my climax as I slowly come back down to earth.

He stands and shrugs off his shirt and pants at the same time I sit up and throw my tee and bra on the floor. As I lean back into the couch, my eyes are drawn down his toned hard body to his cock. When I look back up at his face I'm met with a knowing smirk.

"I think you've had your fun, it's my time now." His voice is low, commanding, calling to me on an instinctive level that I had so missed over the years.

"Yes," I whisper, my throat tight in anticipation of the promise of what Sean can do to me, the way he can make me feel. I can't resist him.

I sit up, needing to touch him. Running my palms over his arms and around his hips, my mouth descends on his cock. I run my tongue across the head, the taste of this man intoxicating. Gripping him with my hand at the base, I wrap my lips around him and suck hard on the tip before lowering down the length of him and sucking my way back up again.

"Fuck, Sammy. I'm no saint and I'm definitely not a superhero with stamina of steel. I need my cock inside you now!" he grates out, grabbing my forearms and lifting me up to my feet, attacking my mouth with an unleashed hunger.

I can do nothing but hold on for dear life as his tongue plunders my mouth. I try to keep up with him, but my mind and body are on different wavelengths. My brain wants to take my time and get my fill of this man, but my body wants everything now. In particular, his rather large cock.

Inside me.

Stretching me.

Filling me.

He pulls away, his hot body against mine too much for my orgasm addled brain. "We don't need safe words, we don't need anything. You say stop, I stop. You say no, I stop. But unless you state otherwise, I'm going to give you exactly what you need, Sammy. I want you to bend over and hold onto the couch and not let go."

My heart races and my breathing hitches as his words, his voice … fuck, everything surges through me. This! This is what Sean offers me, why we click. Why no other man has ever measured up. My knees are shaky as I follow his instructions, leaning over the couch and gripping it tightly as I stand there with my back to him, the anticipation of what he's going to do next threatening to drive me insane. Biting my lip, I look over my shoulder to find him standing directly behind me, looking at me, watching me, and fuck is it hot. The scorching heat in his gaze warms me all over.

"Please, Sean. I need something," I plead wantonly.

I feel his hands glide over the curve of my ass, rubbing the skin in a circular motion. "I love your ass. So firm, yet soft … perfect for my hands. He runs his hands down the outside of my thighs, then back up again, his feather light touch electrifying my body, awakening my senses once more. His fingers glide between my legs, feeling how ready I am for him, and I whimper at the grazing touch.

"Almost, Sammy. Just remember to hold on and don't let go. Do you trust me, sweetheart?"

There is no waver in his voice. No uncertainty. There is nothing but confidence and self-assured certainty in his words.

He is my Dom.

"Yes! Yes, Sean. Please, I need you to touch me."

"Where, Sammy?"

"Anywhere! Everywhere!"

"I am. I will." He leans his naked body over mine, his cock sliding between my legs, resting teasingly against my clit. "I know what you need,

Sammy. Don't. Let. Go," he reiterates in my ear before gliding his hands from my shoulders down my back while peppering soft, wet kisses down my spine, the air cooling the skin in his wake. My body trembles as I wait for him to thrust his cock into me, but instead, I groan as he resumes caressing the globes of my ass, around and around, over and over. Then without warning he lifts one of his hands and spanks me. He fucking spanks me. I lift my head to stand up and feel his other hand pushing me down. My skin burns with heat, the sound of the slap of his hand more shocking than any short lasting pain. I moan as desire shoots directly down between my legs and when I arch my back, raising my ass to him, he chuckles to himself.

"I knew you'd like it. You're a fucking natural, Sammy. Fucking perfect for me." He resumes caressing my ass, my skin alive under his touch as he spanks me again. I lose track of time, my brain switching off as I focus on the pleasure Sean is giving me. My ass feels like it is on fire but so does my yearning for him. "Pleaseeeee," I whine. I know I'm begging but right now my pussy needs his cock like a desert needs the sun. Desperately.

"I know, sweetheart, I know. Believe me, I know," he murmurs as he dips two fingers inside of me. My walls tighten around him and he groans as he fucks me with them, easing the way for his cock. I smile knowing that he's just as desperate as I am, my silence short lived as I cry out in relief and bliss when he removes his fingers, gripping my hips tightly before plunging his cock deep inside me.

He pulls completely out before pounding into me again. "Fuck, I love your tight pussy. I'm not going to last long. I've been hard since the café."

"Don't stop!" I yell as he takes me, over and over until my legs start to shake and I feel lightheaded, another orgasm surging toward me as his grip tightens on my hips, his fingertips biting into my skin.

"Come, Sammy. I want you to come. Now, Sammy!" he roars as he fucks me harder, faster, his cock filling me over and over until he plants himself deep inside me and calls out my name as he climaxes the same time as I do.

I lower my forehead against the couch as I struggle to catch my breath. My legs feel like jelly, but Sean wraps an arm around my waist as he leans over my body from behind once more, his clammy forehead resting against my shoulder as he stays inside me, not wanting to end our connection too soon.

"Better than before," he murmurs as he places a soft kiss against my skin.

"Better than ever," I add.

CHAPTER 17 – "HAPPY"

Sean

Since Sam and I got back together, we've focused on just enjoying each other's company and getting to know each other again. There's been no Ryan trouble, no work stress (well, no more than normal), and no unwanted distractions except each other, so between her shift schedule and my day and night jobs, we've been grabbing every chance we get to spend together.

Earlier tonight I gave her a key to the condo when she came around after work earlier tonight, a gift which she reluctantly accepted. This wasn't because she didn't want it. As she explained it, she didn't want to rush things between us. When I replied that we didn't need to waste any more time than we already had, her eyes softened and she accepted the key gracefully. I ended up pulling her hard against my body and kissing her into submission until her body was soft and pliant against mine, then I proceeded to take her on the kitchen floor while dinner was cooking in the oven. What can I say? I'm a man who can multi-task.

Now it's after dinner (and a shower) and we're both lying on the couch, Sam in front of me, while she watches Criminal Minds (yes, ironic, I know) and I'm reading a deposition. Aren't we just the picture of domesticity?

When the commercial break comes on, I feel Sam wriggle around to face me. "I had lunch with Helen and Rico today." Then there is silence while she waits for a reaction.

I put my papers down in my lap. "Mmm hmm. How is Helen? Still bugging you for details on how good I am between your legs?"

"Sean! No! Well, yes … but no. She was saying how she hasn't seen you since college and how they'd love to meet up for dinner one night."

"Sounds like a great idea. It would be good to catch up."

"You sure?" she asks, sounding skeptical.

"Of course. But why don't we invite them here for dinner instead of going out? We could have it on the rooftop." Her eyes go wide before she grabs my face and pulls me into a kiss, one of her soft, gentle ones that start with her tongue gently tracing my bottom lip before she tentatively moves it deeper. That's all I can handle before I take over control, holding the back of her head as I slant my head and probe my tongue deeper, sliding over hers as I explore her mouth, each kiss a new adventure, another chance to taste her.

I ease out of the kiss, moving my hand down her back and cupping her ass, pulling her hips against my now very hard cock. One kiss and I'm raring to go with Sammy. It's insane, but not unwelcome. "Why don't you invite your partner and his fiancé? We can make it a dinner party."

She looks at me and smiles, her expression one of confused awe. "Are you sure you're real?" she squeezes my bicep, then cups my jaw. "You feel real."

"I'm real … hard right now. Is this enough proof for you?" I roll my hips against hers again, groaning at the friction against my cock.

"You can prove that to me again in about thirty-four minutes once my program has finished." She kisses me quickly before rolling back toward the TV as the program starts again.

I chuckle as I pick up my papers again to continue reading. "You bet your ass I will."

Sam

I shrug on my standard issue, blue CPD shirt over my black, lace, demi bra and panties, quickly checking my watch to make sure I'm still early for my shift. Our early morning shower ten minutes ago had been a vigorous one, starting with Sean lifting me up and wrapping my legs around his shoulders as he feasted between my legs, making me cry out his name—which echoed throughout the condo—before he dropped me back down onto my feet, hooking his arm under one knee and driving into me, making me come apart again before he took his fill. The problem was, I didn't get to do what I wanted to do to him.

Walking into Sean's bathroom, my breath catches as I see the man in question standing in front of the bathroom sink, leaning forward with a hand on the edge bracing himself as he runs his old school, double-edged razor along his rough jaw. Dressed in nothing but a white towel wrapped around his waist he looks every inch the sexy man I know he is. Rivulets of water reflect in the light, and I try to find the restraint to stay away from him.

But where Sean is concerned, restraint is not possible.

I catch his eye in the mirror as I slowly walk up behind him. His green eyes darken as he reads the lust-filled expression on my face. Raising a brow, he silently questions my intent before turning to face me.

"Sammy, what—"

I reach up and place a finger on his lips to silence him before leaning down and licking the irresistible drop of water off his pec. I look back up at him and gently drag my finger down his body, making a trail as I drop to my knees in front of him. "You're killing me here …"

"Not yet, but give me a minute and I'm sure to come close." I slowly pull the towel away from his waist, giving him a wry smile as I come face to face with my most favorite hard body part. My tongue darts out and licks the tip of his cock before I roll the head in my mouth and move down to take his whole length in my mouth. The clean, sandalwood taste of his soap fills my senses as I lose myself in him, sucking and rolling my tongue up and down his satin skinned length.

"Fuck!" he spits out as he drops the razor into the sink, but the loud clatter against the porcelain is muted in my ears as he groans loudly the moment his cock hits the back of my throat, just the way he likes. I feel his hands glide across my shoulders, one tangling in my hair as he tries to regain the control he craves, his other hand cupping my jaw gently as he rubs his thumb up and down my cheek reverently.

I continue to lick and suck his shaft, tracing the large vein running the length of him with the pointed tip of my tongue, earning a jerk of his cock against my mouth as I encircle the tip.

Suddenly he steps back, his hands disappearing. I look up to see him bending sideways, trying to reach his black silk robe. Curious as to what he's up to, knowing that my man's mind works in amazing and calculating ways, I see him pull the silk tie from the robe. The mischievous gleam in his eyes as he looks down at me sends a shiver straight through me. If I thought I was in control, I now know it was all a ruse. Sean is also in control, always waiting to take the next step when he is ready.

He leans down over me, bending at his hips as he runs his hands down my arms until he reaches my hands, gently maneuvering them behind my back. When I feel the silk tie caress my wrists then firmly but comfortably bind them together. My heart starts racing at the realization that now Sean can do whatever he wants with me. And I trust him to do whatever he wants with me, to me … in me.

He runs his thumb gently under the silk to ensure it's safe before running his hands back up my arms, over my collarbone, until he's standing back up to his full height in front of me. His hands cup my jaw and I move forward as he guides his now pulsating cock back into my eager mouth.

"Sammy," he groans as he moves one hand to the back of my head, gently guiding the rhythm. My heart soars as I let him use me, increasing his thrusts until he takes over and fucks my mouth in earnest.

"Fuck I'm going to come in your mouth and you're gonna take it all, Sammy."

"Mmm hmm," I groan my response, my body humming with pleasure as I increase my speed, willing him to fulfill his promise.

He growls loudly and I swallow every last pulse into my mouth, savoring the unique taste that is all Sean.

When I pull back, he lifts me up to my feet, reaching behind my back to free my wrists. Without giving me a second to recover, he tips my head back with my ponytail and kisses me, hard and fast, thrusting his tongue into my mouth in an obvious show of appreciation. His own exceptional show.

Ending the kiss with a soft bite on my bottom lip, he moves me backward and stares deep into my eyes with a sated, satisfied expression. "A fucking fantastic goodbye." His face lights up with a radiant grin, and I realize that ever since I went to his office and abandoned all the resistance I had when it came to him, I've felt happier, content. And as for Sean, I've never seen him so relaxed and carefree … well, as carefree as such an intense, passionate, and measured man like Sean can be.

He takes the time to look me up and down, his eyes blazing with heat when he meets my gaze once more. "Uniform policy change I don't know about?" he asks mockingly with a delicious smirk on his face, bringing out his sole lickable dimple on the right hand side of his mouth.

"Maybe," I say with a wink. "I do need to finish getting dressed and get going." I lean up and place a gentle kiss on his lips before spinning on my heels and walking out of the bathroom, but not before I get a short sharp smack on my half exposed ass that almost makes me want to run back to him and call off my shift.

I said almost.

CHAPTER 18: "DRUNK IN LOVE"

Sam

A few weeks later, we've finally secured a night when we're all available, so I've been busy in the kitchen most of the afternoon, making sure the food is ready for tonight's dinner party. It's the only thing I could do to keep my nerves in check. My best friends and my partner meeting Sean and spending a few hours with us has me anxious as hell.

First, there is Helen and Rico. Helen knows my history with Sean because she was there living it right along with me. From the first time I met him when he infuriated and intrigued me, to my swooning debrief after our amazing first date, through all the highs, and then the horrible low when I broke it off. She's been my drinking buddy, my sounding board, my shoulder to cry on.

She's been there through thick and thin.

Then there is my Brazilian brother from another mother, Rico. He knew Helen and I were a package deal, and since I was friends with them both separately before I played matchmaker, he automatically fell into the role of offering me a male perspective in my life. And by God, have I needed that. He warned me to be careful with Tanner, told me that all the signs were there that Tanner wanted more, but I thought I had it in hand. Well, that backfired didn't it? I haven't heard from Tanner since that night in the club when he stormed off.

And Zander ... well, he's Zander. He's like my other half at work. We've been working together for long enough now that we can anticipate each other's moves, reactions, and share the same instincts. It makes for a great partnership. And after the frequent 'Ice Queen' jokes, I wanted to show him that there is another side to me, the 'out of work' Sam. Although, for some reason he looked shocked, then burst out laughing when I invited him and Kate to Sean's place for tonight's dinner. He wouldn't explain but kept randomly chuckling for the rest of the shift.

I'm just finishing a peanut butter soufflé tartlet for dessert when I feel Sean's arms wrap around my waist from behind, pulling me back into him. He kisses the skin at the top of my spine before moving his mouth to my neck. "You doing okay?" he murmurs softly.

"Mmmm," I moan. His lips leave my skin tingling as he kisses the spot just below my ear, sending a shiver through my body, something his chuckle tells me he didn't miss.

"You need some stress relief again?" he says with a smile I feel against my skin.

"Well, I do need a shower ..." My voice trails off into a moan as he sucks my ear lobe into his mouth.

"Feeling dirty, Sammy?" His teeth graze the skin as his arm around my waist tightens and his very evident arousal pushes against my jeans.

"Very." My voice is shaky. The affect this man can still have on me with a few words is insane. It's like he has a sex thesaurus in his head, with the ability to recall sexy one liners at a moment's notice. "It might be a long shower. Very long. You up for that, Mr. Miller?"

"Cheeky wench." He playfully slaps my ass. "I'm up anytime you need me to be. But for that, you can get undressed right here right now."

I spin around with wide eyes at his sudden commanding tone, the one that makes me wet and ready almost instantly. He meets my gaze with a piercing stare, a 'don't test me' look that makes me quiver in anticipation. "And if I choose not to?" I raise an eyebrow at him, a silent but not well thought through challenge.

He smirks dangerously. "Now, Sammy."

I slowly pull my tank over my head, making sure to draw it out. The growl I hear from Sean is gratifying and well worth the punishment I know I have coming my way. Deciding to up the ante since I'm already in 'trouble', I throw my top in his face and run up the stairs to Sean's bathroom, giggling when I hear him striding behind me.

"You can run but you can't hide, sweetheart."

For the record, he caught me, he had me, he made me scream his name three times straight before he finally bent me over the bathroom cabinet and plunged inside me, bringing on orgasms number four and five.

And yes, it was so damn worth it.

Sean

Sam has been much more relaxed after our mid-afternoon liaison. I was starting to get worried that she was having second thoughts about the dinner party. I'm not stupid; I know that socializing with her friends again is a big step for her. She's taken everything else in her stride since we've been us again that I knew something would trip her up, but so far she's continued to surprise me at every turn.

Last week, I even persuaded her to come to the club with me one night to check on things. With Ryan back on board and Amy taking the reins a bit more at my request, I haven't needed to be there as much. Well, with Sam in my life I haven't needed to be there at all. Of course, she stayed at my side the whole time and even agreed to venture into my private VIP room for a look. Unfortunately for me it was only a look. I'd have loved to have her splayed across my lap, her ass red under my palm before making her come all over my cock in my red leather chair. I didn't miss the biting of her lip and her quickening breaths as she took in the room and the mood shift in the air. I chuckled when she grabbed my hand and pulled me out of there before I tried anything.

Now it's nearing 7 p.m. and time for our guests to arrive. We invited Ryan, but he said he had other plans. He's been a bit evasive over the past week, but I'm hoping it's just a combination of being busy with the bar and therapy while giving Sam and I space to reconnect. Especially since there has been so much reconnecting going on.

I hear the doorbell ring, then watch as Sam rushes down from the bedroom, looking flustered. I grab her arm as she tries to rush past me. "Sweetheart, take it easy. It's going to be fine."

"I … I don't do this. I don't host dinner parties. I'm the single friend who turns up and acts comfortable as a third or fifth wheel, and always with a glass in my hand." She looks at me with those bright-green eyes of hers that always do me in and I instantly feel protective.

"Sweetheart, you don't have to worry about being any kind of wheel now. You have me, and I have you. And besides," I reach behind me and grab a tall vodka tonic, "I already thought ahead." She sees the drink in my hand and smiles widely. "God I lov … like your forward thinking."

I stop breathing for a moment, wishing like hell she would have finished that sentence differently, but instead she quickly takes a big mouthful before putting her glass on the kitchen counter.

"Right, let's go greet our guests, shall we?" I hold my hand out to her and we walk downstairs to the front door together.

"Oh my lord! Girl, you did not tell me he lived in a shrine!" Helen says as I open the door. She hasn't changed too much over the years. She's still loud and outspoken as she always was, and it's still as endearing as it was back when I first met her.

I chuckle as I step forward and kiss her cheek. "Helen, great to see you again."

"You too, Sean. It's been too long." She pulls me in for a hug, standing on her toes so that her mouth is by my ear. "If you hurt her, I'll kill you."

She steps back and joins hands with the man who is watching on with interest. "Babe, this is Sean. Sam's boyfriend?" She looks questioningly at Sam who glares at her in horror.

"Boyfriend suits me," I interrupt. "Although, do we still have boyfriends and girlfriends in our thirties?" I smirk and look at Sam who turns to me in shock. I wrap my arm around her waist and squeeze gently, and she buries herself in my side. Thank Christ.

"Boyfriend," she murmurs quietly as if she's testing the label out. It's fucking cute as hell.

"Sorry, this is Rico, my fiancé," Helen says with a grin.

"Great to meet you. You're a brave man taking this one on."

"You're telling me," he says with a laugh, shaking my outstretched hand firmly and looking into my eyes. He's a straight shooter this man, my kind of guy.

"Hello! I'm standing right here, Enrico. If you want any of this later on, you better tread carefully, mister."

That just makes the rest of us laugh again.

I step aside, taking Sam with me as I gesture for Helen and Rico to come inside. "Come in. We're still waiting for Zander and Kate, but that's not to say we can't start with a drink."

"Now that's what I'm talking about," Helen states as she and Rico make their way up the stairs followed by Sam and me.

I lean down to whisper into Sam's ear, "Your boyfriend would like you to relax, Sammy." She whacks my arm playfully and steps toward Helen who has made herself at home in the kitchen as she prepares drinks.

Rico and I are talking baseball when I hear the doorbell again. I turn to Sam and she waves her hand at me to say she's got it. A few minutes later, the tall blond man and gorgeous red haired woman from the Police

Foundation dinner emerge from the stairs after Sam.

I excuse myself from Rico and walk toward them. "Sean, this is my partner Zander and his fiancée Kate," Sam says, introducing them.

Holding my hand out to Zander, he shakes it rather firmly. "Nice to finally meet you."

"You too. Sam has told me a lot about you," I say to Zander, looking over at Kate and smiling. Her brows narrow briefly before she looks away and sniggers, like there is a joke we're all missing.

His eyes widen briefly before he starts shaking his head. "Now I don't know whether to be worried or whether you're lying. Because Richards here would only talk about me if she were bitching about me. Your woman is a ball buster if you don't already know."

"Roberts ..." Sam growls beside me.

He puts his hands up in mock surrender. "Easy, boss. I'm hoping Sean here is the one who's been melting the ice lately."

I look at him confused before it clicks. "That would be me. Happy to have been of service."

Sam gasps at the two of us before turning to Kate. "He's incorrigible. Would you like a drink?"

"Definitely. I have a feeling we're going to need one," she comments puzzlingly. That's strange. I'm starting to wonder what I'm missing, but it clicks a little while later, during dinner when Sam asks Kate about her day.

"I had a fitting for my bridesmaid dress today. I can't believe they're getting married in the summer."

"I bet you're looking forward to it though. It'll be like a trial run for your own," Helen pipes up.

"Oh, yeah, but Zander and I haven't even started planning our wedding. We need to get Mac and Daniel's one out of the way first."

Oh shit! The strange look becomes all too clear.

Kate knows Mac, she's gonna be her bridesmaid … that would make Kate the best friend …Mac's best friend. Therefore, Kate would know about me and Mac. Ah fuck … now I know what Kate's look was about. She's made the connection already. I tense up when I think about Sam and what her reaction will be. We've had such a good day and now my past is making an unfortunate appearance at what should be an awesome night with new friends.

I grab my phone out of my pocket and send Mac a quick text.

Sean: Kate and Zander are at my house for dinner.

Mac: I know. Kate told me earlier.

Sean: Babydoll, you didn't think to give me a heads up?

Mac: And spoil the fun …?

Sean: That man of yours should spank your ass.

Mac: Maybe I'll ask him to, he's good like that ;) Have fun!

"Sean, is everything all right?" Sam asks from beside me.

"Uh … yeah."

I look down the table to see Kate grabbing her phone off the table and I know I need to tell Sam. I tense up and reach over, grabbing Sam's hand and putting it in my now clammy one just as Kate puts her phone down and turns to Zander.

"Sam, I think there is something you should know."

She looks worried as she looks at me.

"What?"

"Zander and I have a mutual friend …" I wait for a reaction, but she seems nonplussed, shrugging her shoulders.

"Who?"

I reach up and rub the back of my neck, feeling mildly uncomfortable to be doing this in front of company. "Uh, if I'm right, we were both involved with Kate's friend Mac."

She looks over at Zander, then back at me. "I'm confused. That's not unheard of, although it is quite a coincidence."

"Yeah, I only just made the connection. The thing is, Mac had three friends with benefits at the same time …" Then the penny drops. She splutters into her drink, taking a big gulp before putting the glass down on the table. She just stares at me, then turns her eyes to Zander. Kate looks over and bites her lip, like she knows what has just happened.

"Roberts," Sam calls out. "It seems you and Sean have something … sorry, someone in common."

Zander stops talking to Helen and looks over, his eyes full of surprise as he looks at Sam, then me … then something clicks into place and he spits out his drink before flicking me a sympathetic look.

"Shit!" he says under his breath, shaking his head.

"I'm guessing you didn't make the connection either?" Sam asks, her voice light and more casual than I expected.

"Ah, fuck," he mutters, then looks at Kate who is beaming at him as she sniggers, which makes his lips slowly turn up.

My cheeks heat up, and for the first time in twenty years I almost feel embarrassed.

"What am I missing here?" Helen interjects, looking at all of us while Rico just leans back in his chair, putting his hands behind his head like he's just sitting back and watching the show. Lucky bastard.

"Well," Sam announces, "Sean has just realized that him and Zander were banging the same chick at the same time."

"Hang on. At the same time? As in a drunken threesome story?"

I choke on my whisky as both Zander and I shake our heads. "Fuck no!" we both say loudly in unison.

Sam and Kate start giggling and Helen just looks confused. "Hang on, at the same time? As in she was seeing you both at the same time?"

Kate pipes up, her face beaming, "Yep. My best friend Mac was never one to limit herself to just one man. She actually had three friends with benefits at the same time."

Helen slaps her hand down on the table. "Holy crap. I need to meet this girl. That is fucking awesome."

"Women …" Rico growls under his breath which just makes Sam and Kate laugh even more. Fucking fantastic.

"Hang on, that would be like saying Zander and Sean have had sex through association. That's hilarious," she continues.

It's the only time I can say that I wish the world would swallow me up whole.

"Oh my God!" Sam starts saying. She tries to pull her hand out of mine, but I tighten my grip.

"No, no running," I say, my voice automatically slipping into Dom mode.

"I'm not going anywhere, Sean. I just want to get drunk now. The mere thought that you and Zander have fucked the same girl is waaaaay too close for comfort."

"It was almost two years ago, sweetheart. I would've told you had I known. You must know that." I release her hand and run my palm up her arm, rubbing her skin reassuringly. My heart is racing. It's the first time I've actually been afraid that she'd leave again.

"It's okay, Sean. I know you weren't a saint for the past ten years, but now I have an excuse to drink copious amounts of alcohol and have a laugh." She leans toward me, giving me a gentle kiss on my lips before looking me dead straight in my eyes, her lips still touching mine. "And then you can screw my brains out to erase the thought of you and Zander." She moves away and laughs out loud, her carefree attitude contagious as I just look at her and smile.

Fuck, I love this woman.

I look over at Zander and he gives me a grimace before I lift my chin, making sure he knows that everything is okay. Kate sees us and loses it again, leaning into Zander's side and laughing.

Rico speaks up, thankfully changing the topic. "Dinner was awesome, guys, but you know me and my sweet tooth, Sammy. I just know that your dessert is going to be epic."

An epic dessert to conclude an epic dinner party.

Definitely one for the books.

CHAPTER 19: "HEY BROTHER"

Sam

I'm in a deep sleep when I'm woken up by a phone ringing. My body feels like a dead weight in the bed as I struggle in that wonderful no man's land between being awake and being asleep. I roll over and look at Sean's alarm clock beside the bed, grumbling at the fact it's only 3 a.m. and someone is calling us.

Sean's arm wraps around my waist and I snuggle deeper into his side. There is something about burrowing into a nice warm hard body that is comforting, and arousing. Fuck! How can I want to go again when he only just finished with me a few hours ago? I must be an addict. Addicted to Sean Miller. Fuck, if this keeps up we'll end up screwing each other to death. On the bright side, what a way to go!

The phone starts ringing again and I hear a growl rumble in Sean's chest. "This better be fucking good," he mutters as he moves away, sitting up against the headboard and shifting to reach the phone.

He sighs before answering the call. "Ryan, this better not be what I think it is."

My body goes tense as I think of all the possible reasons for Ryan calling his brother in the middle of the night.

It's been four months since I came back into Sean's life. Four fantastic months without drama, without Ryan fucking up, and without middle of the night phone calls. This can't be good.

"Mmm," Sean hums, listening to his brother. I sit up beside Sean, resting my head on his shoulder. I can only hear a jumble of sounds coming down the phone, but when Sean's body goes deathly still, I know it can't be good.

"You're fucking shitting me, Ryan. Ten thousand?" The room is suddenly quiet. Sean is breathing hard and I know he's trying to control himself, but after the last time Ryan was beaten up in the club, Sean's patience for his brother is all but run out.

"What the fuck do you expect me to do, Ry? It's not like I have ten grand in cash just lying around my house …"

More silence, more noise down the phone.

"He said what? Oh, fuck this shit. Ryan, you made your bed and I told you that I was done with this crap, but that bastard has gone one step too far now." I sit up straight and watch Sean's features, his jaw twitching as he grinds his teeth loudly. "Where am I going?"

I jump out of bed and throw some yoga pants and a hoodie on, foregoing a bra and panties because there is never much of a need for them with Sean around. I turn the bathroom light on and go to the sink to wash my the sleep out of my eyes.

I look at Sean in the mirror, feeling his penetrating glare. Shaking his head, he breaks his gaze. "Okay. I got to get dressed and sort Sammy out. Then I'll be there. Tell the bastard I'm on my way. And Ry … do what you have to do to stay safe, all right?" He nods his head and my breathing hitches.

Ryan is in trouble. Serious trouble.

"Yep, okay. See you soon."

He slams his phone down onto the bed and stands up, stalking naked toward me. "Sweetheart, I know you got the gist of that conversation, but you need to get back to bed."

"No, Sean. I'm a cop. This is what I do. I can help."

He continues advancing on me until his naked chest is touching mine. "Sammy. It's because you're a cop that I'm telling you that you need to step down and get back into bed. This is my business. Ryan has been fucking up for as long as I can remember. It's not the first time I've tried to get him help, and it's definitely not the first time he's relapsed. He's got himself into a bad situation and I'm going in to get him out of it. They've threatened him, and they've threatened the club, then they got stupid and let him get ten thousand dollars in the hole. Without the money, he has nothing to play with. He's run out of cards and run out of luck, ten fucking years too late. Now, they threatened me and my 'cop' girlfriend, and that's one step too far."

"Sean!" I implore, resting my hands on his chest. "I have to call this in. It's my duty. They've threatened us, and your brother is at risk. One call and I could have a team raiding the place in an hour."

His eyes bore into me. "No, Sammy. No cops, no calling it in. You are NOT getting involved in this. I can't allow that."

I step back, banging my hip into the bathroom vanity. "You can't allow that? Like I'm some errant teenager who needs to be put back in her place? Fuck you, Sean. You cannot control my job. Control me in the bedroom, yes, but NOT my FUCKING JOB!" I yell at him. My job has always been a no go zone for anybody involved in my life. Not even my mother has been allowed to meddle in my professional life. Hell, I haven't let my mother meddle in my life full stop since I realized she had cost me Sean.

He puts his hands on my shoulders and steps in close to me again, crowding me. "I'm not ordering you. I'm telling you that you can't get involved. I don't want to put your job at risk, and this situation, this backroom poker table that Ryan is sitting at, is not the place for an off duty police officer."

He steps away and turns back toward the bedroom, dressing quickly before grabbing his wallet, keys and phone from beside the bed. "You're taking your car?"

"Don't have a choice. It's the middle of the night and I'm not going to use a town car to pick up my brother from god knows where in the car service. I'm just going to grab him and get him out of there, then send him to fucking Timbuktu or Siberia until it blows over."

I storm back into the bedroom, stopping on the opposite side of the bed. "Sean, it doesn't work like that. I've dealt with shit like this before. They won't stop coming after Ryan until the debt is paid, usually with interest. And when they can't find him, they'll target the club, they'll come after you at the firm, and then they'll come after me. It's not a case of getting him out of there and this blowing over." I wave my arms around dramatically, trying to explain the ignorance of Sean's plan. He walks around the bed and puts his hands on my hips, pulling me in tight against him.

"I'm not going to argue with you about this. You're staying here, I'm going to get Ryan and drop him off at a hotel for the night. You'll wait for me here, naked in my bed …" He kisses my jaw, then my nose, then stops at my lips, slowly teasing me with his tongue until I relent and give up my resistance, moaning as he languidly explores my mouth.

"You don't play fair," I grumble when he pulls away. Another quick brush of his lips against mine and he is all business.

"Get back into bed. I won't be long."

"Where are you going? Someone should at least know where you're going in case it goes to shit."

"It's a rundown bar off West North Ave in Austin. He said they're in a room at the back. Sounds classy right?" He laughs sarcastically. "Sam, go back to bed. I'll be back before you know it."

Having already decided what I'm going to do, I nod my head at him. His eyes go soft as he looks at me one last time. "Good night, sweetheart."

And with that, he turns and walks out of the bedroom. I listen as his footsteps get further and further away as he goes down the stairs to the second floor, then down the two flights of stairs to the basement parking garage.

Sitting down on the bed, I rest my head in my hands as I struggle to compose myself enough to do what I have to do. What I must do.

I grab my cell off the bedside cabinet and stare at it, cradling it in my hands as I contemplate the consequences of what I'm about to do. I didn't lie to Sean when I said my job was non-negotiable. If a crime is being committed it is my duty to call it in and protect people. Or in this case, the man I love and his brother who, despite being an idiot who doesn't learn from his past mistakes, I also care about.

I couldn't live with myself if something happened to either of them and I could have stopped it.

Scrolling through my contacts, I pull up my friend Jeremy's number. He's a detective at my precinct who has been investigating illegal gambling and was also involved in investigating the robbery at Throb until I told him discretely what really went down, then the case was wound up quickly. There was no need to keep it open when there was no robbery and no way of identifying the assailant. But I've since found out that Jeremy had been heading an investigation into a string of illegal gambling events reportedly being organized and held in the Chicago city area, so I know that he is the person to talk to about whatever Sean is heading into.

"Richards, what the hell? It's 2 a.m. and you should be sleeping or fucking. Or a bit of both. What gives?"

"Jeremy, Sean just got a call from his brother. He's in trouble at a backroom poker table in an Austin bar. Sean told me not to call it in, but I had to call you. If it's that same bookie that roughed him up a few months ago, then who knows what might happen. What should I do?"

"Shit, Sam. I'm at my desk, but I can grab some officers and try and get there, but there are no promises that I can protect Sean in this. It'll be a blanket arrest, then weed out the bad from the good after that. You okay with that?

"Anything. Please, Jeremy. I can't sleep knowing him or Ryan could get hurt."

"Okay. I'll call you back in a while once we get the lay of the land. What bar?"

"I don't know. He just said it was off West North."

"Ah yes, I know exactly where. We'd been staking it out up until last week. Gotta go. Keep your phone on. You'll hear from either me or your man."

The call ends and I feel my stomach tighten. I feel sick. If I've overreacted … Why the fuck is it the middle of the night and why the hell isn't Helen working a night shift.

I go downstairs and turn on Sean's very expensive coffee machine, pacing the kitchen as I wait for the liquid gold to brew. With my now full cup in my hands, I walk over to the couch, bending my legs up close to my body as I stare out the window waiting for word from Sean or Jeremy.

The problem is that, as a seasoned cop, I know the city never sleeps. There is always a criminal element that comes out at night, making itself known … or not if they're smart. Men and women are robbed or attacked, cars are stolen, houses are broken into, illegal poker games with high bets and even higher stakes are played. Kingpins preying on the addicted few, desperate to win their money back, adamant that their next hand will be the one that takes them back into black again. But it never happens. Lines of credit are offered and accepted, and soon enough, like Ryan is right now, they're staring down the barrel of an even larger debt.

My fingers tighten around the warm ceramic cup in my hands. Ten grand! Ten fucking grand! Who lets themselves get that far into a hole in one fucking game? Don't get me wrong, ten years in the department and I've seen it all. Doesn't mean I can't be surprised when it happens to someone I thought knew better, or had at least learned their lesson from last time.

I wouldn't want to be Ryan when Sean gets his hands on him. I had to intervene last time when Sean said he'd washed his hands of his brother. This might just be the straw that breaks the camel's back. If not that, then I might have just stepped over the line myself. I can only hope that Sean realizes the position I was in and can forgive me.

CHAPTER 20: "THE MAN"

Sean

I slide my black Maserati into a parking spot opposite the bar where Ryan said he was. From the outside, it looks like a standard upmarket Chicago cocktail bar. I shake my head and check the address again, looking for some dodgy warehouse or something more fitting for underground gambling. Surely this can't be right. Illegal gambling should be held in a rundown, hole-in-the-wall bar that looks like the health department will be knocking on the door any day now. Nothing like this scene in front of me.

Knowing that Ryan's phone will be on silent, I have no option but to find him myself. Getting out of the car, I set the alarm and stroll across the street, noticing with interest that the bar is closed and a few staff are the only ones left inside as they pack away for the night. I check the neighboring premises and see that there is an alleyway around the side of the building. Knowing that Ryan is inside somewhere and in trouble, I waste no time in crossing the street and walking down the alley, checking constantly for anyone following or coming out in front of me. I'm not worried about having to defend myself; it's more the surprise factor. I'd rather be on guard than be caught unprepared, and since I came unarmed, I may be at a disadvantage.

I see an old wooden door at the end of the alleyway with a rather large black man guarding the door.

"You Sean?"

"Yep."

"Got ID? Can never be too careful."

"Right. I pull my wallet out of my back pocket, showing him my license. He hands it back to me and steps forward, pulling the door open. "You better be here to bail your bro out. He's in trouble. So far in the hole he's losing sight of the light, if you know what I mean."

I swallow hard. Fuck! I lift my chin to the guy before stepping inside, the hazy, smoke-filled room stifling as I walk toward a large round table. Checking the table and not seeing Ryan, my eyes go to the guy leaning back in his chair at the head of the table.

"Where's Ryan Miller?"

"You his banker?"

"What the fuck do you think?"

"You got his money? He said his brother was coming and would sort it all out for him. We put him somewhere safe until it was all taken care of." The smarmy man smiles, his mouth full of big, overly white teeth. It's almost creepy, and I'm a hard man to rattle.

"You think I can pull that kind of money out of my ass at 2:30 in the morning? You know as well as I do that most law abiding citizens don't have that kind of dough lying around. So I give you my word that the money will be paid into your account as soon as the bank opens."

I just hope Ryan isn't in so much trouble that I can't save him. I may be pissed, but he's my only family. Ryan and Sam are the only ones who matter to me. Why do you think I didn't bring her along? It wasn't because I didn't think she could handle herself, but I refused to put her in a position where she would have to defend herself or put her job on the line. She loves her career too much for that.

The Cheshire cat starts laughing, slamming his palm on the table, seemingly finding the situation hilarious. "See, mister lawyer man, here's the thing. I know you think you've got a leg to stand on, and I don't doubt that

160

you're packing some big kahones down below, but I don't give a fuck." The smile on his face fades and he glares at me, his eyes almost venomous. "I'm trying to run a business here. I don't operate credit without collateral or without knowing that I can get the money back from somewhere. Your brother has a big mouth when he's desperate. He says you own that hot place in the club district and that you've got a hot piece of cop ass for a girlfriend. That was all the collateral I needed because I knew you wouldn't put her in hot water, unless she's just a piece of ass—"

"You shut your fucking mouth. Leave her out of this," I spit out, clenching my fists at my side as I try to rein in my anger, knowing I just fucked up and gave him what he was gunning for.

He smirks at me, knowing he has my back to the wall. "So we have an understanding. Fifteen grand tomorrow morning 10 a.m. or else I start causing trouble for you and your little girlfriend. I bet she's hot, too. What do you think, boys? You think a hot shot like this guy would have a tight piece?"

The three guys flanking him start murmuring to each other, agreeing with him if their nods are any indication.

"Ryan said ten grand."

"It's now fifteen." For fuck's sake! "Deal. Now bring Ryan out here and we'll go."

"Maybe I should keep him as insurance—"

His threats are cut off by a thud against the door and the splintering of wood behind me as suddenly the words, "Chicago PD!" ring out and I'm pushed against the wall, face first, my hands held forcefully behind my back.

"Don't say a word," a stern male voice mutters in my ear. Not being stupid, I shut my mouth. I feel the cold metal of handcuffs wrap around first one wrist, then the other, as my hands are shackled behind my back.

I hear a scuffle behind me as more officers pour in. "There's another room back here," an officer calls out to the others. "Shit, there's more of them."

"My brother, he's back there!" I shout, my voice muffled.

"We know what we're doing, Mr. Miller, so I suggest you stay silent. I'm taking you back to the station where you'll stay until we can ascertain your part in all of this."

"You know I'm a lawyer, right?"

"Don't care. Right now you are a suspect in an illegal gambling racket that we've been investigating for a long time. Lawyer or not, I recommend you keep your mouth shut."

I clamp my mouth shut as I'm pulled back by my arms and pushed out of the door and up the alley like an everyday common criminal. Just as one of the cops undoes my handcuffs and stuffs me into the back of a waiting patrol car, I turn my head and see a worse for wear Ryan being led by another officer to the car behind me. His eyes meet mine and I can see the guilt residing there. His shoulders are drawn up and there's none of his normal cocky swagger that Ryan's known for. Just as he is about to disappear from sight, he looks back up at me and mouths 'I'm sorry' before the officer puts a hand on top of his head and ushers him into the back seat of the car.

When the patrol car I'm in pulls away from the curb, I shake my head and stare out the window. After a few minutes, the detective in the passenger seat turns around and faces me.

"I'm Jeremy, lead detective on this case. Samantha Richards called me an hour ago and informed me that there was a poker game going on that I would be interested in and that she was concerned for the welfare of you and your brother—"

I shoot him an incredulous look. "Sam called it in?"

He nods his response and I clench my fists. My Sammy, the woman I left in my bed to come save my brother's ass, ignored my request and called it in anyway. I shake my head in disbelief.

"She was worried that you would get hurt, especially if it's the same bookie that assaulted your brother last time. She did the right thing, Mr. Miller."

I trusted her to listen to me. I told her not to call, that I'd let her know if I needed help. She didn't trust me to deal with this myself. She didn't believe that I could do it without her help.

My anger simmers under the surface as we pull up outside the precinct. It continues to fester and eat away at me as I'm led inside to an interrogation room. I don't see Ryan arrive; in fact, I don't see him again.

After being read my Miranda rights, I explain everything that went down from the moment I received Ryan's call, to recounting everything the asshole bookie said to me, including his threats against me, the club, and Samantha. The detective grows antsy when he hears Sam's name mentioned.

When I'm released clear and free a few hours later, the sun is just starting to rise. A patrol car droops me back at my car which thankfully was still parked outside the bar.

But instead of driving straight home to Sammy, I drive to the club, park at the back and go straight to my office where I become acquainted with a nice bottle of 1800 tequila that I swiped from the bar.

   ***

Around noon, I'm woken up by my ringing phone. When I see Sam's name on the screen I reject the call, knowing I owe it to both of us to sort my head out before talking to her or else I'll likely say something I'll later regret.

Who says history never repeats?

They lied.

Sam

I wake up with a stiff neck, the sun shining straight in my face as I unravel myself from my curled up ball on the living room couch. Checking my watch, I realize I fell asleep and I don't know what has happened. I jump up and run upstairs to the bedroom, expecting to find Sean and coming up short when I can't find him anywhere. Running back down to the kitchen, I pick up my phone and ring him, getting his voice mail all five times.

Fuck! What if he's lying in a ditch somewhere? Or sitting in the cage with real criminals?

I bring up Jeremy's name and bring the phone up to my ear.

"Yo."

"Jeremy. Where's Sean? What happened?"

"Slow down, cupcake. He's fine. I released him a few hours ago. He was dropped back at his car and I assumed he was headed home. He didn't show?"

My breath hitches. Sean didn't come straight home. My hand starts to tremble as I realize that Sean must be livid. He's never been one to shy away from confrontation, and he's not the type of man who lets problems fester. If he is angry, annoyed, frustrated or simply just pissed off, he deals with it. He's direct and to the point, and he never avoids dealing with an issue. He just does it. It's his way. This enduring strength is one of the things that has always attracted me to him.

Now I feel like an imposter in his home. If he didn't want to come home, that means he didn't want to see me. Then, like a Mack truck, it hits me.

I need to leave.

"Jeremy, what about Ryan?"

"His case wasn't as straightforward as Sean. He was participating in the game and he knows a lot about the bookie we're trying to build a case against. He's clammed up at the moment though, which isn't helping him or us."

"You need me to talk some sense into him?"

"It's out of your jurisdiction, Sam, and if the captain got wind of it, you could be accused of interfering in the course of justice. What I will say is that right now, Ryan is in a holding cell but could be moved to an interrogation room with the cameras off if someone wanted to come visit him, check on his welfare shall we say."

I breathe out a sigh of relief. "Text me what room and when. I'm heading down there now. Give me twenty minutes and I'll be there."

"Sounds great, cupcake. And don't worry about Sean. I know a thing or two about these big, proud, dominant types. He'll come around and see that what you did was for the best. Just give him time."

A lone tear trails down my cheek as his words sink in. I can only hope that what he says is true.

CHAPTER 21: "AM I WRONG?"

Sam

I walk into the station, nodding to the desk sergeant as I walk up the stairs toward the interrogation room where Jeremy told me Ryan would be waiting.

Jeremy is waiting in the corridor, his lips pressed together in a grimace as I walk up to him. He looks at me for a moment, his eyes full of concern as he tries to gauge my mood. "You good, Richards?" he asks.

"I will be once I knock some sense into that dickhead's skull. I need to scare him straight, Jer, and the only time to do that is going to be right now without his domineering, overzealous older brother breathing down his neck. Right now I'm neutral between the Miller boys, although I am a cop so I can make sure he understands just how bad this might get." He nods and I continue. "Did you talk to the DA?"

"Amazingly, he took my call and was surprisingly receptive. You get Ryan to agree to testify against the bookie, about the whole damn racket, and he'll be granted immunity and will escape the third strike. I'm sure he doesn't need to be told what will happen if he fucks up again?"

I shake my head and smile at Jeremy before wrapping my arms around his back and squeezing tight. "I'll never be able to thank you enough for this," I whisper in his ear. I step back and look at him, uncharacteristic tears gathering in my eyes.

"You keep up this human behavior, Richards..." I gasp in shock and glare at him. " ... and I'll tell all the guys you're really a girl." He winks at me and I whack him hard on the arm.

"I'm different at work, you know that," I explain.

"Yep, and you wouldn't be half the cop you are without that hard exterior. What I'm trying to say is that it's nice to see what's underneath coming out. Your friends know it's there, and I'm sure that your man and his brother definitely know it's there, and it just might pay to let it shine more often. You won't be seen as weak, you know. Just the opposite."

"Quit it before I cry. It'll ruin the tough cop wake-up call I'm about to deliver in there." I jerk my head toward the closed interrogation room door and he chuckles.

"Right. Be quick though. The Captain doesn't know about it yet. Ryan will still need to give me a statement after you've gone, but anything he says to you is off the record and off camera. Comprende?"

"Got it. Thanks, Jer. I owe you one."

"Hell yeah, you do. Just bring in some donuts or something. You know I struggle to maintain this figure." He rubs his slightly rounded stomach and grins.

"Deal."

He turns and walks away from me as I face the door and slowly take a deep breath. I reach out and turn the knob. Stepping inside, I swear I can see the wide eyed, messed up twenty year old from ten years ago. The one living in his big brother's successful shadow. The one who lost his parents young, then lost his beloved grandparents just as he was getting his life back on track.

But now isn't the time for excuses. Ryan needs help, and I'm going to be the one to give it to him.

"Sam," he breathes out, his voice relieved. I barely have a minute to sit down before he speaks. "Have you see Sean? Is he okay? Please tell me he hasn't been arrested?"

I close my eyes and struggle to compose myself. Ryan doesn't care about himself right now; his only concern is Sean. "Ryan, Sean was released without charge this morning. He didn't come home, but he has his car, so I guess he's gone somewhere to calm down."

"Calm down? Is he that mad with me?"

"Probably," I reply with a shrug. "But it's more likely that he didn't expect me to go against his wishes and call it in, which is probably more unforgivable in his eyes because he didn't see it coming."

"You … you called the cops?"

"I am a cop, Ryan. Something you might've forgotten but I can't. It's my job, it's my career, and if I know a crime is being committed and that two people I care about are in danger, I will do everything in my power to avoid that. You don't think I'd let you get hurt do you, Ryan?"

"Well … no, but I told you I was going to try and get help. I told both of you. And I have been. I've been going to Gamblers Anonymous and meeting with my therapist twice a week. It's just that when I got wind of this table, I thought I could make some money and start to pay Sean back. Do you know he paid off the bookie and paid my rent up to date last time? I didn't even ask. He wrote me off, told me that he was cutting ties, but then he went and did that."

My eyes soften as I listen to him. "He loves you, Ry, but right now he's pissed the fuck off. But it's more than that. You can't worry about Sean because you're in a hole that you can't get yourself out of unless you make the right decision, and you need to make it quick because there's an offer on the table that will give you a chance at a life. A legal, free life."

His body stills as my words sink in. The room is quiet except for a lone clock on the stone wall ticking away the seconds. Ryan wrings his hands together. "You need me to testify, don't you?"

"Immunity from prosecution in return for your testimony on the gambling, the assault at the club, the game last night, and anything you have seen or heard that would strengthen the DA's case."

No hesitation, no wavering. He shocks the shit out of me when he looks me dead in the eye and answers immediately. "I'll do it. Where do I sign? What do I have to do? I can't go to jail, Sam. I can't do this again. I need help, major help, but I want to stay straight. I want to make you and Sean proud. I want to do it for Granddad and Grandma, for Mom and Dad. I need to do this to make everything right."

I see the wet sheen of tears in his eyes and I know that he's been scared straight. Something has sunk in this time and I release the breath I've inadvertently been holding in.

"Please help me, Sam. I need to do this. No more fucking up, I thought I was invincible and my stupidity almost got Sean arrested. I need to make it right. If doing this, if testifying will help me do that, then bring in the detective, bring me the papers, I'll sign whatever they want."

I reach over the table and place my hand over the top of his hands. "Ry, Sean loves you. He wouldn't have left his bed in the middle of the night and told me not to do anything if he didn't love you. You're doing the right thing. For you especially."

I stand up and look at him one last time before opening the door and walking out. When I reach Jeremy's desk, his eyes lift to meet mine and one chin lift is all it takes to answer him.

"I'll take care of it, cupcake. You let me know when you find that man of yours."

"Will do, Jer. Thank you. For everything."

"Anytime. Now get out of here before the captain sees you and starts asking questions. You're a good cop and an even better woman. Everybody sees it."

Unable to speak without losing it, I nod and walk away from him, though this time I feel like I'm walking toward something rather than running away.

When I call Sean's phone later from home, I end up leaving a message on his voice mail, telling him everything he won't let me say directly. I lay it all out, put my heart on the line and tell him I'll wait to hear from him.

What else can I do?

Sean

I leave my phone on my desk, not willing to answer it just yet. My head is throbbing and my mouth feels like I've been sucking on a slimy dish rag. Not my finest moment, I'm sure. I go down the corridor and have a quick shower, throwing on some clothes I found in the gym bag in my office before I sit behind my desk again, resting my head in my hands and willing the Advil to start working.

My phone beeps with another missed call. I pick it up, swiping the lock screen open and see the voice mail icon flash up at me. Gritting my teeth, I call my service and wait for the message to start replaying.

"Sean, it's me. I know you were released this morning and I know you were dropped at your car. You obviously know that I called my friend Jeremy and asked him to do something to help you last night and I'm guessing that's why you didn't come home to our bed, to me …"

She called it home. She called it our bed.

"… I know you're angry at me, and part of that is warranted, but most of it is not. I did what I had to do as a cop who knew that something illegal was going down and as a woman who knew that the man she loves was going into an unknown, possibly dangerous situation."

She loves me. Fuck! My heart swells. I knew it, but to hear the words again from her own mouth … nothing can describe it.

"I know what can happen in those backroom games, Sean. I've done stints in

narcotics and organized crime, and I knew that you were going in there unarmed and without back up which is stupid in that kind of scene. Jeremy has been investigating underground gambling, heading a city wide task force and working toward bringing these guys down. What happened last night has helped him, a lot. I've already been down this morning and talked to Ryan. We managed to get him a deal in exchange for his testimony. He escapes his third strike and he's promised me that whatever it takes, he'll do it."

Crap. In all my anger, I didn't even think about it being Ryan's third strike. My fist clenches tight and slams down on my desk. I was too closed off, furious with him for screwing up again after so many promises of getting his life sorted to think about the consequences for him. Three strikes would have meant jail time, a lot of jail time. The thought of my brother locked up is like a punch to the gut.

"Anyway, I hope you get this and that you'll come see me when you've cooled down. I hope you can see where I was coming from and that, given the situation, I had no other option. I'm a cop. I can't turn a blind eye when I know a crime is being committed, and I wouldn't have been able to forgive myself if something had happened to you or Ryan. I love my job, but I also love you, Sean. I've always loved you. I was just in denial. But I'm not hiding from it anymore. I want you, I want everything you can give me and more. I want to give you me—my body, my heart, everything. I hope you're still willing to give me the chance."

Fuck. I'm a pig headed fool.

I stand up suddenly, having to brace myself on my desk as residual dizziness threatens to drop me on my ass. Once the room stops spinning, I push the car service speed dial on my desk phone, ordering a car to take me home as soon as they can get one to me. Swiping my keys off my desk and putting my cell in my back pocket, I lock up the club and make my way out to the front where I wait patiently for the car.

I try to call my home phone to no avail before trying Sam's cell. It goes unanswered and I hang up before leaving a message. What I need to say needs to be said face to face.

The town car pulls up and I settle in the back seat before telling the driver where to go. Home to my girl.

Sam

It's nearing two o'clock in the afternoon. I finally have a missed call from Sean, but he didn't leave a message, so I'm not getting my hopes up until he calls back and I actually hear from him.

I've been thinking back on the past four months. Our relationship has been so much easier this time around once I admitted the truth to myself and to Sean. Had I just talked my doubts through with him back when we were first together, we could've had a real shot, but I naively listened to my bent out of shape mother and let her twist Sean's need for control into something ugly and not true. Instead of being able to thrive under his hand and blossom under his dominance in the bedroom, I threw it all away and hid. He was never trying to control and dictate my life. He cared about me.

He loved me.

So when I left that message on Sean's voicemail this morning, I let everything hang out. I laid it all on the table, not wanting to have the excuse of miscommunication to fall back on. I wanted him to know where I'm coming from and how important my job is to me but also, how important he is to me too. I get the call from Jeremy that Ryan is free to go and that he needs to be picked up. Driving him back to his apartment, he was very quiet, almost contemplative, until I pulled up outside his building. "Ryan, make sure you get something to eat, then some sleep. I don't think you got much of that in the cage." I smile warmly and his eyes get some of their sparkle back.

"No, I don't think it's possible," he retorts.

"Tomorrow, you need to call your therapist and make another appointment. And I meant what I said a while ago. I'll come to your GA meetings if you need me to. I'll sponsor you if that will help."

"I'm sorry, Sammy. I really am."

"I know, Ry."

"Tell Sean I'm sorry."

"You can tell him yourself. That's if he ever comes out of hiding."

"He'll be at the club, probably locked away in his office. He'll come to you when he's calmed down. You'll see."

"Glad one of us is confident."

Before getting out of the car, he leans over and puts his hand on my shoulder. "My brother never got over you, Sam. He never got another girlfriend, and he sure as shit didn't get married. He's been all about his career, the club, and obviously bailing me out of shit. Now it's time for the both of you to get your happily ever after. He'll come round."

"I hope so."

With a gentle kiss goodbye on my cheek, he gets out of my car and walks into his apartment building. I drive home to begin the waiting game, which didn't end up taking that long.

Sitting on my front step when I pull into my driveway is the elusive man I love.

CHAPTER 22: "LET'S STAY TOGETHER"

Sean

Sam steps out of the car, her eyes cutting straight to me as she takes slow, almost cautious steps toward me, her pursed lips the only sign of her wariness as she sidesteps me on the steps and unlocks her front door.

"Come in." Her words are soft and unsure, like she's trying to brace herself for whatever is coming.

"Sammy, I—"

"Let's get inside first, Sean. I'd rather have a coffee in my hand before we start talking. I'm guessing by the look of you that you've had about as much sleep as I had which isn't much."

I follow her inside her apartment, then shut the door behind me as I watch her drop her purse on the kitchen counter and head straight for the coffee maker. She turns it on before reaching up and pulling two mugs from the overhead cabinet.

"I just dropped Ryan home. He's feeling pretty sorry for himself, so I told him to grab something to eat and catch up on sleep." She's talking really fast, but her voice is steady and matter of fact. "And Jeremy has talked to the DA and the deal is set in stone. Ryan just has to keep going to GA and meetings with his therapist, then testify against that guy who had him last night. You'll probably have to testify against him too, but Jeremy didn't tell me much about what you guys talked about." She's so damn nervous that she's rambling, talking a million miles an hour. "And I offered to be Ryan's sponsor for GA if he wants me. Otherwise, I said I'd attend meetings with him if he needs me to. Whatever he needs, I'll do it."

She stops talking but continues to stare at the coffeemaker. I'm cemented in place, leaning against the back of her couch, facing the kitchen. I hear her take a deep breath, almost like she's bracing herself for something, before turning around and walking over to me, holding out a hot cup of black coffee. Looking up, I offer her a gentle smile which she returns.

"Thanks, sweetheart."

I watch as she walks around and curls into the chair in the corner. I follow her around the couch, sitting on the edge of the gray, suede three-seater so that I can stay close to her. I hate the emotional distance stretching between us, like she doesn't know how to act around me all of a sudden, like we haven't been virtually living together for the past few months, touching each other, loving each other …

I look at her, taking her in. Her sandy blonde hair is pulled back off her face, her high ponytail accentuating her high cheekbones and soft jaw line. Those gorgeous green eyes that I lose myself in daily … those biteable pink lips that I can't wait to taste again …

First things first.

"Did you mean what you said?" I ask, refusing to let her pull away from me again.

"What?" she asks, her voice emotionless.

"Your voicemail. You said you loved me. Did you mean it?"

Her eyes widen minutely before narrowing, like she can't believe I'd ask such a thing. "Of course I meant it, Sean. I meant every word I said."

She leans forward, putting her cup on the glass coffee table in front of her before standing up. I look up at her and tighten my fingers around my mug as I fight the urge to grab her hips and bring her closer to me.

Bringing her hands up, she rests them on my shoulders, running them along my collarbone and cradling my neck. All of the tension that has been steadily building throughout the day dissipates and suddenly my whole body relaxes. Her eyes soften as she feels my muscles loosen under her touch. I decide that now is the time to swallow my stubborn pride and accept that the beautiful woman standing in front of me was right in doing what she did. She stood her ground and stuck to her guns. How can I ever be mad at her for that? She literally saved my ass by calling the cops. Now I can't hold back.

I place my hands on her hips, looking up at her. "Sweetheart, I'm sorry." She nods, her eyes softening as I see a spark of something in there. Something good. "I'm stubborn and I'm an idiot. I went to the club and got smashed on tequila instead of coming to you. I should've come straight home, but I was pissed off. I told you not to call it in and you did."

I flex my fingers, inching them under her T-shirt so that I can feel her silky skin against mine. I stand up so that we're on an even keel. "I love you too," I say, leaning forward and brushing my lips against her mouth, my eyes locked with hers. I pull back slightly. "I've always loved you."

I slide my hands under her top, cradling her back and pulling her chest hard up against mine. This time I run my tongue around her lips before slowly pushing inside her mouth when her lips part on a moan. Her hands snake through my hair, her grip tightening amongst my strands. I pour everything into the kiss. All the heat, the passion, the bedroom tricks I have … none of it means anything in this moment. It's about Sammy, the woman I love, finally admitting what I suspect are long held feelings.

Pulling back, I rest my forehead against hers. "Am I forgiven?" I ask with a sly grin. She smiles, her lips twisting into a mocking smirk.

"I suppose I'll keep you around."

I laugh. "That's good then. But I think we've still got a problem …" I stand up straight and rest my hands back on her hips again, pulling her away slightly so my cock can come down from its seemingly permanent rock hard state.

"What?" she asks, her head jerking back in surprise.

I look around her living room, noticing how warm and homely it feels. "There are quite a few things in this room that would look awesome at the condo ..." I wave one of my hands around, pointing at the couch, the chair, the old oak bookcase she has full of books. "That bookcase would look great in my office." I stand up and turn toward the couch I was just leaning against. "This couch is much more comfortable than my leather one."

She takes a step back from me so that my hand slips off her waist. "You want to take my stuff and put it in your condo?" Her hands are resting on her hips and her stance is definitely that of a pissed off woman.

"Well, yeah ..." I joke. I fight back a grin as I watch warring emotions cross her face. Deciding to put her out of her misery, I step toward her, crowding her against the wall. "I'd hope you would want to bring your stuff to my condo since you're moving in." I give her a hard and fast kiss before walking toward the bookcase, perusing the books like it's my god given right. There is a method to my madness, believe me.

"Oh, hell no."

I school my face to look serious as I turn around to face her once more.

"You can just hold up right there, Sean Miller. You do not come into my house and declare that I'm moving in with you without asking me nicely. No fucking way. You can boss me around in bed, but you can never just decide what is happening in my life without asking me first. Fuck no!" Her eyes are breathing fire as she glares at me, and I know that this is the woman I want forever.

I stride over to her, pushing her with my body against the living room wall, holding her cheeks in my hand as I thrust my tongue in her mouth and kiss the shit out of her. I pull back just enough to wrap my hands under her firm, jean clad ass before lifting her up, her legs instinctively wrapping around my hips as I carry her through the doorway leading to her bedroom, then turn and drop back onto the bed, bouncing against her and causing an eager whimper to escape her mouth.

"Say yes," I murmur against her neck as my lips lay wet kisses against her skin.

"Fuck yes," she says, her voice breathy and uncontrolled.

Couldn't have said it better myself.

CHAPTER 23: "UNDER CONTROL"

Sam

It's been a month since I've moved in with Sean. Thirty days of domestic bliss.

Well, almost.

He seems to love riling me up just to have the hot make up sex that follows. It's almost predictable now. That's not to say I don't let him get away with it. It started off with little things—dirty dishes left in the sink, arguments over the need (or the lack of need) for a housekeeper now that I'm living with him ... oh, and Sean's absolute refusal to let me pay rent. THAT was a good one. I ended up with my legs tied spread eagled to the bed, my hands still free to roam as Sean straddled me, first my face, then my hips, teasing and torturing me until I gave in and agreed to buy food, but not pay rent. Instead, he offered to accept payment in on call sexual favors. That earned a slap against his chest and a scowl which earned me orgasm denial for a full hour until I was screaming at him to make me come or let me do it myself.

Now it's a Thursday night, and having just got off my shift, I head straight to the club where Sean has told me he will be catching up on paperwork. Sneaking through the back entrance with my key, I make my way up the staff stairwell to the VIP floor, walking down the long dark corridor until I get to the black enamel door at the end, knocking three times before stepping inside.

"Sweetheart, you're early," he states as he looks up at me leaning my

179

back against the door. His brow furrows as he takes in the view. "And still in uniform?"

I tilt my head and look at him. "Didn't think you'd complain but I can go if you want …" I shift to my right toward the door handle and I see him smile.

"No need to get hasty. I'm not quite finished yet, that's all." His voice is laced with amusement and the knowledge that he knows he called my bluff. Damn him. I decide to up my game. It is his birthday after all, and birthdays are all about treats and surprises.

"I'll just sit on the couch and wait, no bother." He quirks an eyebrow and watches as I kick my shoes off and pad across the carpet, leaning back leisurely on his black leather couch putting my work bag beside me.

"I won't be much longer," he explains.

"That's okay. I have some time." I smile sweetly at him. With a quick shake of his head, he returns his attention to the papers on his desk, switching between them and what looks like reports on his computer screen.

I grab my bag, pulling back the zipper and reach inside, finding my handcuffs and my F21. Time for the games to begin.

Sitting back against the couch again, I put my index finger inside one arm of the handcuffs and twirl them around my finger, the glint of the shiny metal and the rattle of the chain enough to capture Sean's attention as he first turns his head, then his office chair around so that he's facing me. Even from ten feet away I can see the outline of his hard cock in his slacks, his legs spread and open (for comfort more than anything) and all of my plans leave my mind as I'm overcome with the desire to sink to the floor between his legs, unzip those pants, and bury his cock in my mouth.

"See something you like, Sammy?"

"I think you might like what's in my hands better, Mr. Miller." I give him a saccharine sweet, innocent smile and he growls as his grip on the arms of his leather office chair tightens.

"What's in your other hand, Sammy?"

"Oh, just my standard issue F21 expandable baton. You know, the one I really shouldn't have brought home with me. Oops." My voice is full of high inflections, a mock innocence that just makes the knowing grin on Sean's face widen.

He stands up and stalks toward me, stopping when he is standing above me, his eyes dark and foreboding, full of heat. "Do you need to be punished?"

"Well, since I took it for your birthday, I think it's only fair." I giggle, totally exposing my plan within five minutes of being with him. I'm a hopeless case!

Holding out my hand to him, he wraps his fingers around my wrist like a cuff and pulls me up, bringing my body flush with his, my soft meeting his hard. Simply divine.

"I love your dirty plans, Sammy. But as you say, you must be punished. And it is my birthday after all. Shall we head home then?"

I hesitate, too nervous to tell him what I really want to give him for his birthday. The one thing I've been holding back on since we came back into each other's lives. "I ... I want to go to your VIP room, Sean."

He freezes as my words sink in. "Sweetheart, you don't have to do this for me. I don't need that room anymore. I have you, and I love everything we do and everywhere we do it."

I rest my palm against his cheek. "I want you to take me to your VIP room, Sir. I want you to do what you want to me, with whatever you deem necessary. I'm leaving myself in your hands, leaving everything at your discretion, Sir."

Sean

If I thought I was hard before, it was nothing to the intense throbbing I feel in my groin right now. Not only has Sam shocked the shit out of me by pulling out her handcuffs and her baton, she wants me to take her to my private VIP room, to take her at the club, something I thought she was so vehemently against that I haven't even raised it as a possibility.

"You sure?" I ask, my face full of concern. There is no way I'm going to do this if her heart's not in it.

She looks at me and smirks, her eyes full of mischief as she hands the handcuffs and baton to me. "I've been a bad girl, Sean. I need you to take me to your room and spank me."

Fuck.

Like a shot of heat straight to my dick, that's all the confirmation I need. I bend down and throw her over my shoulder, carrying her through my office door as she shrieks in surprise. I hold her still, swatting her ass hard as she squirms against me. "Behave, Sammy," I growl as I pull out my set of keys from my pocket and open up the door to my right, walking in and slamming the door behind me before reaching over and flicking the lock.

I lower Sam's feet to the floor, running my hands up either side of her body, tracing her curves as I run my palms over her breasts. The quick rise and fall of her chest gives away just how breathless she is, and I'll bet everything I have that she's wet and ready for me already. My need to have her weighs heavy on my mind, but there is still the small matter of her 'punishment' that I must dish out. It is my responsibility, you know.

"Strip," I order, standing in front of her with my arms across my chest.

Her hands rush up to undo her shirt, letting it drop to the floor as she unhooks her bra, then undoes her uniform pants and bends down, taking her black thong off with them before adding to the pile of clothes beside her.

Feathering my hands down her arms, I wrap my fingers around the implements held tightly in her fists, smirking when she resists giving them over to me. "Tut tut, Ms. Richards. This was your game plan all along, and I'm going to make sure that we follow it through. You stay there for a moment, Sammy, while I decide where and how I'm going to take you. No moving, no turning around. I want you to watch yourself in that mirror on the door. Don't look away. I want you to look and see the woman that I cherish, the beauty I worship, and the body that every man covets, but will never have." My command is deep and penetrating.

She nods her head, her breathing picking up as the anticipation starts to affect her in the most exquisite way. Her nipples are hard tempting peaks, and her legs are steady but a little shaky.

Walking around her, I put the baton down on the small table beside my beloved red leather chair which I'll be considering moving to my condo since I'm going to be giving up this room to another paying client. But that can be the good news I tell Sam about after we've finished enjoying my birthday present.

Hooking the handcuffs to my belt, I saunter toward her, locking eyes in the mirror over her shoulder as I advance on her now trembling body. "Sean," she whimpers and my hands go straight to her hips, my palms rubbing against her skin in slow circles as I brush her ponytail aside with my nose, gently pressing my lips to the nape of her neck. I feel a tremor run through her body, and I smile as I run my mouth across her skin, peppering a line of kisses to the spot just below her ear, meeting her heated, almost desperate eyes in the mirror.

"Fucking beautiful, sweetheart. Best birthday in years because I'm here with you." I run my hands inward, my gaze dropping to my fingers as they glide their way along her pelvis, delving into the juncture between her thighs. She drops her head back onto my shoulder, a moan echoing around the room as I brush my thumbs against her slick pussy. I pull back as I bare my teeth and bite the soft skin along her collarbone.

"Fuck!" she spits out, her voice barely a whimper. My hands slide up over her stomach until they're cupping her breasts, the heavy weight beyond temptation as I roll my thumbs over her hard nipples, squeezing just enough to see her eyes drift closed as waves of pleasure roll through her body.

I run my hands down to her wrists, encircling them with my fingers, and slowly pull them in front of her, holding them in place with one of my hands while the other unhooks the cuffs from my belt and captures first one wrist, then the other until both of her hands are locked in place against her stomach and I can easily run a finger around the inside of each cuff.

"Turn around, Sammy," I ask and she complies beautifully. The way in which she gives herself over to me is still such a heady experience and a gift I honor every single time.

Her eyes are glazed as they lift up to mine, her head muddled, her equilibrium off balance as she acclimatizes herself to the scene we're playing. "It's time for your first punishment."

"First?"

I run a finger along her hairline, then across her cheek until I catch her lower lip and pull it down. "First and last, sweetheart. I want to feel your skin under my palm. I want to hear the anticipation catch your breath as you wonder where my hand will strike next." Her eyes flare with lust and I know she's totally on board with this 'punishment'. We both know that it's no more of a punishment than it is a prelude to the mind blowing pleasure to follow soon after.

"I need you to stand over there and bend over the side of my chair. Then you're going to stretch your arms out in front of you, gripping the other side until I tell you otherwise." She closes her eyes and groans, not shying away from her body's almost automatic reaction to my heated words.

Unable to resist even the smallest of tastes, I grab her ponytail and pull it back sharply, slamming my mouth down on hers and thrusting my tongue deep inside. A growl reverberates between us as I taste and take from her, her lush body melting against mine in gratifying supplication.

I pull away, and satisfaction surges through me as her eyes slowly open, softly gazing up at me as I offer a sly grin. "Now, Sammy."

She saunters over to the chair, the soft sway of her naked hips a seductive taste of the pleasures to come for both of us.

Once she's followed my instructions to the letter, I walk up behind her, pressing my straining cock against her bent hips. I strip off my shirt silently, building the anticipation. When I lean my bare chest over her back, lightly resting against her, her breathing becomes labored until she is panting beneath me, her ass writhing against my dick. I place my hands on top of hers, slowly trailing her now extended police baton along her skin, leaving a swath of goose bumps in its wake as the cold metal drags over her shoulders. Running the tip down her spine, she trembles with need as I inch closer to her ass, then rolling it over the swell of her ass, I tap it a few times expectantly, not missing the erotic moan that caresses her lips. I continue down the back of her right leg, pressing into the dip of her knee until it circles her ankle and travels up the inside of her legs, slowing to an impossible pause at the apex of her thighs and sliding through the slick wetness gathering there before continuing its descent down the other leg.

My own breathing quickens as I bend down to the floor, spreading her feet wide as I lay the twenty-one inch baton between them. "You're not to move your legs back together, Sammy. I want you to hold this baton between your feet and no matter what I do or what your body instinctively wants you to do, you will not close your legs to me. Do you understand, sweetheart?"

"Yes," she whispers hoarsely, the desperation in her voice like music to my ears. She's right there with me, desperate for more, aching for my touch, my mouth, my hands, my cock.

Needing her more than my next breath, I kneel behind her and move my hands back up her body, firmly and with purpose as my fingers edge closer to her wet core. I move my head between her legs, suddenly burying my tongue deep inside her sopping wet pussy, the scream that escapes her mouth spurring me on as I spear her repeatedly before running my mouth lower and sucking my lips hard over her hard clit, tapping it with the flat of my tongue until she cries out my name, her climax taking her by surprise as aftershocks wrack her body around me.

Standing back up to my full height behind her, I run my hands back over her ass, rubbing wide circles over her now sensitized skin. "Sean, I … I don't know if I can handle more."

I quickly undo my slacks, pulling them down along with my boxers and kicking them off to the side with my feet. "You can and you will. For me, for my birthday. I want to see your ass glow red under my hand before I sink my cock deep inside your pussy. I want you to beg for me, begging for me to make you come."

"I need you now, Sean. More than anything in this world," she whines as I resume the slow circles over her ass cheeks.

"Patience, sweetheart. You know that I love delayed gratification. Ten years I waited for you. Ten years I waited for this." I lift my hand up and bring it down quickly and firmly, slapping my palm against the pale soft skin of her ass, her scream of shock and pleasure ringing in my ears as I rub over my red hand print soothingly.

"More," she moans, tilting her hips toward mine. I bite my lip to stifle a groan before spanking her on each cheek in quick succession, running my index finger down the seam of her ass and dipping between her legs and coming back soaking wet.

"You're enjoying this, sweetheart. You're dripping for me. Your body is glowing for me."

She whimpers with need as I run my fingers around her clit with feather light precision, teasing and taunting her in the most intimate way. "Seannnnn," she whispers my name and fuck if I don't feel it right down in my cock.

"You'll take more, Sammy. I want you on the edge when I sink inside you. When your walls clamp down around me." I trail my index finger firmly over her clit before running it along her slit and right back over the curve of her reddened ass.

Bringing back my hand one more time, I flatten my hand and deliver another blow, more stinging than those before. She screams out my name and I need to touch her. I lean over her back, the heat radiating off her skin searing my legs as my hard dick nestles into her ass crack. I kiss her shoulder in a gentle, open-mouthed kiss that causes her body to tremble with need.

"I need you as bad as you need me. Tell me how much you want me, Sammy. How desperate you are to have my cock …"

"Please, Sean. I can't stand it. I need you inside me." The desperation in her voice unmans me and I lose any resolve I still had left to draw this out any longer.

"Fuck it," I mutter through gritted teeth as I pull my hips back, lining my cock up with her entrance and surging forward, plunging deep inside her, the slap of our skin the most satisfying sound in the world apart from my name being chanted by the beautiful woman beneath me like the most reverent benediction.

I pull back and thrust back inside, repeating over and over until my fingers bite into her hips and Sam's head is thrashing side to side on the chair as her climax strangles my cock. We cry out together, crashing over the crest with an intensity only ever experienced with each other.

Slowly stroking my cock inside her, I collapse against her back, struggling to catch my breath as I come back down to earth.

Best fucking birthday ever.

Best fucking woman in the world.

And she's all mine.

EPILOGUE

Sean

I pace backward and forward along the living room floor, stopping briefly to check my watch before resuming my nervous gait. I roll my thumbs over the top of one another, my clammy hands clasped in front of me. My stomach tightens and turns as my mind wonders at all the possible outcomes.

I hear the click of the front door and the thud of Sam's gym bag as it hits the bottom landing. Fuck, this is it. The moment in a man's life when he lays it all on the line, balls and all, offering them up to the woman he loves. Entrusting her with his heart and soul for the rest of their lives.

Shit, is it too soon? Will she think I've lost my mind and laugh at me? I roll my shoulders and walk over to the window, my view over the park calming me down slightly as I hear her footsteps on the stairs get louder as she nears the top.

I check my watch again. 10 a.m. Helen will be arriving at noon. I can't rush this, although I can't wait to ask.

Look at me now, the big bad Dom humbled by his potty mouthed sexy as hell sub girlfriend. I've never done this before. Never wanted to do this before. Never even fucking considered it, and now I feel like a nervous wreck.

I wring my hands together and close my eyes, taking a slow deep breath to try and calm myself.

For the past week, this day has been all I could think about. Will she or won't she? Can I pull this off? Have we had enough time together this time around to make a real go of this?

Lost in my anxiety, I feel Sam's warm hands wrap around my chest, her breasts pillowed against my back as she rests her cheek on my shoulder.

"Good morning," she murmurs as my hands cover hers and hold her to me.

"Morning, sweetheart. How was your workout?"

"Good, although I can think of many more enjoyable ways to build up a sweat. Most of them involving you …"

I chuckle at her forwardness. It's taken awhile for us to get to this point. I love that she owns her sexuality and doesn't hide behind it. I love that she yields to me willingly and trusts me to give her exactly what she wants and needs.

I love that outside of that, she's strong-willed and confrontational, that she meets me toe to toe when she wants to and knows that I respect the hell out of her for it. On the flip side, I love that she's caring and thoughtful, always willing to help out her friends and colleagues. I love that when push came to shove, she put herself and her job on the line to clear my name and help Ryan get out of the shit he'd put himself in. I love that she waited for me to get over myself and accept that I'm not alone anymore.

"I love you," I say softly. When her breath hitches, I know she's heard me. Every time I tell her that, she reacts the same way. It's like she still doesn't quite believe that we found each other again.

I remove my hands and turn in her arms, meeting her eyes head on when I do. They're wide and filled with tears. She places her hands over my heart, her fingers fisting in my shirt as she continues to stare up at me. I cup her jaw and bend down, kissing her lips softly before moving back.

"I love you, Sammy. I knew the moment I saw you again. I knew the moment I stood on your doorstep before dinner. I knew when you entered the ballroom for the foundation dinner. I knew when you gave yourself to me again even though you were shit scared that you'd get hurt. And I knew the moment you put your job on the line to save my ass ..."

"Sean, I—"

"Sammy, I've loved you for eleven years. Not once have I stopped. I always remember the way my mother looked at my father. They were so in love, they weren't showy or in your face about it, but it was evident for everyone to see. They lived and they loved, then they died together. I want to live my life with you, I want to live the rest of my life in love with you. I want to love you so much that you look at me with adoration and trust, with love ..."

I step away from her, reaching in my pocket and pulling out the black velvet box that has been burning a hole in my pocket for the past hour. With trembling fingers, I open it and reveal my mother's sapphire and diamond channel set engagement ring. I bend down on one knee and look up at her, her bright green eyes now glistening as tears roll down her face.

Reaching out for her left hand, I grasp it tightly as I swallow down the lump in my throat, my own eyes growing damp. "Samantha Grace Richards, will you grow old with me? Will you be the mother of my children and make me the happiest, sappiest man on the planet? Will you marry me?"

She bites her lip and pauses, the silence deafening as my world stops spinning waiting for the one word I want to hear. The word I need to hear.

"Yes," she says hoarsely. I pull the ring out of the silk encasing and slip it on her ring finger. She drops to her knees and crushes her body against mine, our lips meeting feverishly as we attack each other with renewed passion. "I love you so much," she mutters against my lips before I run my hand through her hair and pull her ponytail, exposing her neck to my mouth as I trail kisses down her throat.

"Fuck, I need to be inside you right fucking now," I growl. I lay her down on the rug in front of me, surrounded by the light streaming in the window from the Chicago skyline. I rip down her leggings and underwear, throwing them out of the way before hovering over her body and kissing her mouth, sliding my tongue against hers as I roll my hips against hers. She moans loudly which just fires me up even more.

She reaches down and fumbles with my belt, undoing it and my jeans before pulling them down just enough for my rock hard cock to spring out. I open my eyes and watch her as she spreads her legs for me, her eyes full of heat as I thrust inside of her, planting myself to the hilt, relishing the feeling of being inside my fiancée, the love of my life.

Bucking her hips against mine, I slide all the way out before pushing back hard inside of her again, her moans echoing through the room. Her hands snake around to grab my ass, her fingernails digging into the bare skin. We take our time as I worship her body in every way I can. Knowing that she is mine for the rest of my life has calmed me. I take my time to kiss her, the languid strokes of my cock amping up our bodies until we climax together, her body tightening around mine, milking me for all I'm worth as we slowly come back down to earth.

"I'm the luckiest son of a bitch in Chicago," I announce with a grin as I stroke her hair away from her face, getting lost in those jade green eyes of hers.

"That makes me the luckiest girl then doesn't it, fiancé," she replies gently.

"I kind of have one more surprise for you, Sammy."

She furrows her brows, her hands resting on my face as she struggles to pull her eyes away from the gorgeous antique ring on her finger. "More than this?"

"What would you say if I said that I want to marry you today?"

Her body goes rigid beneath me, her voice shaky when she can speak again. "How? We'd need a license first, and then there is the one day waiting period."

I love that she knows this, but lucky for me I've already thought about all of that. I grin down at her, our bodies still intimately joined as my hips slowly move backward and forward, my cock starting to harden again.

I lean my head down and run my tongue along her bottom lip. "We can have the ceremony here today, then go down to the courthouse Monday morning. I've already made an appointment for us. Then we go back on Tuesday and get married in front of the Justice of the Peace, making it all legal."

I pull back and watch her eyes go hazy again. "But today, in front of our friends, I am going to pledge my love and my life to you. For richer or poorer." Kiss. "In sickness and in health." Kiss. "Till death do us part …"

I kiss her hard, devouring her mouth and robbing her mind of coherent thought as I pour everything I have into that one kiss. By the time I lift my head, she is nodding through tears again.

"Fuck, I love you, Sean Miller."

"I know," I say with a shit eating grin on my face. "I take it that's a yes?" I ask with a quirked brow.

"It's a hell yes! But wait, I don't have a dress or anything."

I chuckle, my body rocking against hers which earns a whimper from Sam. "All taken care of. But first …"

I thrust my hips against hers, my cock rubbing against her G-spot, sending a shudder through her body. Once again we lose ourselves in the moment as I take her on the floor of our living room, not stopping until she's writhing beneath me, giving herself to me intimately, a physical acceptance of my proposal.

And let's be honest, it's kind of expected that I'd take my wife-to-be just hours before our wedding. It's just my way.

Sam

Helen fusses over me as I smooth my hands down the white satin wedding dress. Helen explained to me that Sean came over to her place a few weeks ago and explained his plan. That he would be proposing to me in the morning, and by 2 p.m. we'd be married on his rooftop in a civil ceremony, to be followed up by a legal ceremony at the courthouse on the first available day afterward.

Helen was in charge of choosing our flowers and our outfits. Sean knew that Helen would be the next best person other than myself to choose the perfect wedding dress and he was not wrong. The dress is a bias-cut, satin slip gown with a low draped back, a sweeping V neckline and gorgeous, embellished, lace sequins adorning both shoulders. The smooth satin feels exquisite against my skin with my barely there lace thong the only underwear possible under the dress. My hair is a wave of loose golden curls flowing down my bare back, pulled off my face by a matching lace sequined hairpiece, and to complete the look Helen has done my makeup soft and natural.

I feel like a princess.

A girly, feminine, sexy princess who is about to go marry her dominant prince charming. The one man who has always been her all.

"Oh shit."

"What, Sam? Shit, did I forget something?" she asks, her face suddenly full of concern.

"What about Mom? I guess she's upstairs. I swear to god if she causes ANY grief today, I'll lose my shit."

Helen looks at me, suddenly looking tense, almost awkward. "Ah …

yeah, about that …"

"What?"

"I made an executive decision. She doesn't deserve to be here today. Not for you, Sammy. You can be pissed at me, I probably deserve it but I didn't want anything to ruin your wedding day. Legal or otherwise." She looks at the ground, probably the only time in our thirteen year friendship that Helen has been meek and unsure of herself.

Fuck I love this woman.

"You are the BESTEST friend I could have ever asked for."

"What?" Her eyes snap up to mine. "You're not mad?"

"Fuck no! She would probably block the aisle just to stop me from getting to Sean. Screw that! Nothing is stopping me today. Absolutely nothing." I step forward and give her a huge hug which she returns before pulling back.

I grab Helen's hand and look at her watch. 1.55 p.m.

Shit. I'm just minutes away from one of the most memorable moments in a woman's life. I feel the flutter of butterflies in my stomach, but for once, I'm not worried. I'm not even nervous. I'm excited. I look over at Helen and smile brightly at her.

"Babe," she says, her eyes going soft. "If you don't cut that shit out I'm going to start crying again and then I'll ruin my makeup, and nobody wants to see that. So quit it!" she says with a smile just as there is a knock on the bedroom door.

She rushes to the door just as it starts to open. "Oh no you don't, Mr. Mill … oh. Hey, baby," she coos, kissing Rico as he walks past her. He comes up to me, stopping a few feet away and scanning me from head to toe. "Você está linda," he says softly, calling me beautiful, and I know he's itching to hug me.

"Don't you start, Rico, or else I'll start crying, then Helen will start crying, and we'll all be a right mess!"

He chuckles, reaching into his pocket and pulling out a long, white jewelry box. "Well, I think you might cry anyway, Sammy. This is a wedding gift from Sean. He told me to tell you 'it was always meant to be you' and that you'd understand the significance."

I bite my lip, trying to control my emotions. Rico hands over the box and my hand trembles as I open it up to see the most exquisite, white-gold diamond and sapphire necklace I have ever seen. I run my fingers over the pendant, a large, bright-blue sapphire which matches Sean's eyes perfectly, encased in a circle of small diamonds, then surrounded by a circle of small sapphires again.

Rico steps forward and removes the necklace from my hand, looking at me questioningly before I nod my head, still trying to hold back the unshed tears that have filled my eyes. I turn around and carefully lift my hair off my shoulders as he places the pendant around my neck and secures the clasp. Lowering my hair, I walk over to the mirror and stare in awe at the sparkling jewel that has completed my wedding attire perfectly. Now all I want to do is run upstairs and tackle hug my future husband. That's allowed, right?

Rico clears his throat to get my attention. "Sam, Sean has asked me to give you away today. Would you let me have the honor?"

I smile before rushing over to him and hugging him. "Of course, Rico. It's perfect. My two best friends walking me down the aisle to the man I love."

"Oh, God, that's done it. Now I'm going to look like a drowned raccoon. Thanks a lot, babe!" Helen pipes up behind us, her voice cracking.

Five minutes later, Helen's makeup is restored to its previous pristine condition and Rico opens the door, leading us down the corridor and up the stairs to the rooftop.

As we pause at the top of the stairs, I hear the murmured voices of people talking, then a sudden silence just before the music starts playing. Helen gives me a long stare full of unspoken words of support and love, before kissing my cheek and whispering, "Twenty-five percent of people don't have sex on their wedding night. Buck the trend," in my ear. I burst out laughing as she winks at me, then spins around and disappears from view as she walks down the aisle.

I take a deep breath and feel Rico gently squeeze my hand reassuringly as the wedding march starts to play.

"This is it, baby girl. Time to marry your man."

And that is all I need to hear as Rico and I step forward around the corner and lock eyes with my beautiful man dressed in the most stunning tux I have ever seen.

I'm marrying the man I love, the only man I've ever loved. The only man who has seen the real me and who has taught me to embrace it.

The only man who has ever been it for me.

Sean

The music starts and my eyes are riveted to the open rooftop door, waiting for the first glimpse of the woman who will become my wife.

Helen has already walked down the aisle and beamed at me, her gorgeous, forest-green dress skimming the floor as she walks to the side of the celebrant and turns to face the crowd.

Then my heart literally stops beating in my chest as I see a wave of white satin flash through the door.

"Wow," I hear Ryan murmur beside me but I dare not look away. I don't think I could even if I wanted to. I'm too mesmerized by the vision walking toward me. She looks stunning … no, she looks exquisite, delectable, beautiful. My feet itch to meet her halfway down the aisle just to make sure she gets here faster.

I've battled her, I've pushed, provoked and fought for her, and I know in this moment I'll continue to fight for her until my dying day. I'll love and protect her, shield and support her, and wake up every morning knowing that I'm the luckiest son of a bitch to have her.

My Sammy.

My Blissful Surrender.

Epilogue song – "Be My Forever" – Christina Perri & Ed Sheeran

Next up Dr Noah Taylor aka The Walking Dildo
and his story in
Finding Bliss – Winter 2014

<u>Bliss Series Order:</u>
Temporary Bliss (Bliss #1)
True Bliss (Bliss #2)
Blissful Surrender (Bliss 3)
Finding Bliss (Bliss #4)

Crave by BJ Harvey

I have a craving.

A dark urge that I've failed to resist despite years of trying to do that very thing.

I've forced myself to hide behind a mask, a perfect orchestration to hide my true self.

After I met her, my wants and needs, my inner most desires changed.

She encouraged me to embrace who I truly am, and she was willing to do anything and everything I wanted, giving herself to satisfy my most carnal appetite.

Then everything in my carefully managed world came crashing down around me. A moment in time, a loss of control, and the very thing I cherish was nearly taken from me.

My fate now lies in her hands.

The very life I've built for myself…everything I've ever done now waits in purgatory, all caused by a lack of focus at a time when my most concentrated attention was needed.

The very thing I crave may now be the very end of me.

Coming Fall 2014

About BJ Harvey

BJ Harvey is the Amazon Bestselling Author of The Bliss Romantic Comedy Series and The Lost Romantic Suspense Series. An avid music fan, you will always find her with headphones when writing, and the speakers blaring the rest of the time. She's a wife, a mom to two beautiful children, and a full-time university student. BJ resides with her family in what she considers the best country in the world—New Zealand.